An hour before midnight the inn closed and its lights went out.

The darkness was black; the stillness was interrupted only by occasional rumblings of distant thunder. . . . The two adventurers crept toward the inn. Huck stood sentry as Tom felt his way into the alley. The longer Tom was gone, the more fearful Huck became. It seemed that hours had passed. Tom must have fainted, Huck thought. Maybe he was dead. Maybe his heart had burst with terror. Huck fearfully approached the alley. There was a sudden flash of light, and Tom came tearing by. "Run!" he cried. "Run for your life!"

A Background Note about
The Adventures of Tom Sawyer

Tom Sawyer shows what life was like in a small Missouri town on the Mississippi River in the 1840s. In such a town—located in both the Bible belt and the slaveholding South—prejudice was the norm.

Mark Twain mocks the religious intolerance he witnessed as a boy. For example, he comments on a student composition that "concluded with a sermon so damning of all non-Presbyterians that it won first prize." Clearly, Twain disapproved of "pious" people who literally damn to hell anyone with different beliefs.

Like religious bigotry, racism runs deep in the world of *Tom Sawyer*, where whites feel superior to Native Americans and blacks. Tom's friend Huckleberry Finn critically refers to "Injun" Joe as a "half-breed." And Huck considers himself generous for treating an enslaved black man, who has been kind to him, as an equal. "I don't ever act as if I was above him," Huck remarks. "Sometimes I've set right down and ate *with* him."

Ironically, while Huck looks down on Native Americans and blacks, most whites look down on *him* because he is poor, homeless, and uneducated. In *Tom Sawyer* prejudice comes in many forms.

THE ADVENTURES OF
TOM SAWYER

MARK TWAIN

Edited, and with an Afterword,
by Joan Dunayer

 **THE TOWNSEND LIBRARY**

THE ADVENTURES OF
TOM SAWYER

TP **THE TOWNSEND LIBRARY**

For more titles in the Townsend Library,
visit our website: **www.townsendpress.com**

Townsend Press, Inc.
1038 Industrial Drive
West Berlin, New Jersey 08091

ISBN 1-59194-025-7

Library of Congress Control Number:
2003116575

PS
1305
.A38
2004

TABLE OF CONTENTS

Chapter 1

"Tom!"

No answer.

"TOM!"

No answer.

"I wonder what's goin' on with that boy. TOM!" The elderly woman pulled down her eyeglasses and looked over them around the room; then she pulled them up and looked out under them. She rarely, if ever, looked *through* them for as small a thing as a boy. The eyeglasses were her fancy pair, the pride of her heart, built for style, not service. She could have seen as well through lids for a stove's burners. "I swear, if I get hold of you, I'll . . ." She didn't finish because she was bending down and jabbing under the bed with a broom, and she needed breath to put strength into the jabs. She roused no one but her cat. "I never did see the equal of that boy!"

She went to the open door and looked out

over the weeds and tomato vines that formed the garden. No Tom. She raised her chin to an angle calculated for long-distance calling and shouted, "Y-o-u-u, *Tom*!"

There was a slight noise behind her. She turned just in time to seize a small boy by his jacket, stopping his flight. "There! I should've thought of that closet. What've you been doin' in there?"

"Nothing."

"Nothing! Look at your hands. And your mouth. What *is* that stuff?"

"I don't know, Aunt Polly."

"Well, *I* know. It's jam. I've said forty times that if you didn't leave that jam alone, I'd skin you. Hand me that switch."

The switch hovered in the air. "Oh! Look behind you, Aunt!"

Aunt Polly whirled around.

Tom instantly fled, scrambled up the board fence, and disappeared over it.

His surprised aunt stood still for a moment. Then she laughed. "Hang the boy," she thought. "Ain't he played enough tricks like that on me for me to be wary of him by now? Old fools is the biggest fools. But, my goodness, he never uses the same trick twice. He seems to know just how long he can torment me before he gets my dander up. And he knows that if he can get me off guard for a minute or make me laugh, my dander will go back down and I won't be able to hit him even once. I ain't doin' my duty by that boy. That's the Lord's truth. But he's my own dead sister's boy, and I ain't got the heart to lash him. He'll play hooky this afternoon, and I'll be obliged to make him work tomorrow, to punish him. It's mighty hard to make him work Saturdays, when all the boys is having a holiday, but he hates work more than he hates anything else, and I've *got* to do some of my duty by him, or I'll ruin the child."

Tom did play hooky, and he had a great time. He got back home barely in time to help Jim, the small black boy owned by Aunt Polly, saw and split the next day's firewood before supper. That is, Tom was there in time to tell Jim his adventures while Jim did three-fourths of the work. Tom's younger half-brother, Sid—a quiet boy with no adventurous, troublesome ways—already was done with his part of the work (picking up chips).

While Tom was eating his supper, and stealing sugar to the extent that opportunity allowed, Aunt Polly asked him questions. She wanted to trap him into revealing that he'd played hooky. She flattered herself that her attempts to deceive were marvels of cunning. "Tom, wasn't it hot in school?" she asked.

"Yes, ma'am."

"Didn't you want to go swimming?"

Tom felt an uncomfortable suspicion. He searched Aunt Polly's face, but it revealed nothing. So he answered, "No'm. Well, not very much."

Aunt Polly reached out and felt Tom's shirt.

"You ain't hot now, though." She was pleased with herself: without anyone knowing her intention, she had discovered that the shirt was dry.

Tom realized what was happening and forestalled Aunt Polly's likely next move. "Some of us pumped water on our heads. Mine's still damp. See?"

Aunt Polly was annoyed to think that she had overlooked that evidence. Then she had a new inspiration. "Tom, you didn't have to undo your shirt collar, where I sewed it, to pump on your head, did you? Unbutton your jacket."

Tom opened his jacket. His shirt collar was securely sewn.

"Well, go along. I was sure you'd played hooky and been swimming." She was half sorry that her shrewdness had miscarried and half glad that Tom had, for once, been obedient.

Sid said, "I thought you sewed his collar with white thread. Now the thread is black."

"Why, I did sew it with white! Tom!"

Tom didn't wait for the rest. As he went out the door, he said, "Sid, I'll wallop you for that." He thought, "She'd never have noticed if it hadn't been for Sid. Sometimes she sews my collar with white, sometimes with black. I wish she'd stick to one or the other." Sid was the town's model boy, so Tom hated him.

Within two minutes Tom forgot his troubles—not because his troubles were one bit less heavy and bitter to him than an adult's are to an adult, but because a powerful new interest drove them from his mind. This interest was a new way of whistling that he had just learned and was longing to practice. It consisted of a bird-like warble produced by touching the tongue to the roof of the mouth. Reader, if you ever were a boy, you probably remember how to do it. Through diligence, Tom soon got the knack of it. He strode down the street whistling.

The summer evenings were long, so it wasn't dark yet. Tom stopped whistling when he encountered a stranger, a boy slightly larger than himself. A newcomer of any age or either sex was an impressive curiosity in the shabby little town of St. Petersburg. And this boy was well dressed, on a *weekday*. His cap was dainty. His buttoned blue jacket was new and stylish. So were his pants. He had shoes on, although it was only Friday. He even wore a necktie, a bright bit of ribbon. He had a city manner that ate into Tom. The more Tom stared at the boy, the shabbier he felt and the higher he turned up his nose at the boy's finery.

Neither boy spoke. If one moved, the other did too—but only sideways, in a circle. The two boys stayed face to face and eye to eye.

Finally Tom said, "I can lick you."

"I'd like to see you try."

"Well, I can do it."

"No, you can't."

An uncomfortable pause. "What's your name?" Tom asked.

"It isn't any of your business."

"Well, I'll *make* it my business."

"Well, why don't you?"

"If you say much, I will."

"Much, much, *much*."

"Oh, you think you're smart and fancy."

Another pause. More eyeing and sidling around each other. Now they were shoulder to shoulder.

Tom said, "Go away."

"Go away yourself."

"I won't."

"I won't either."

They stood, each with a foot placed at an angle as a brace, and shoved at each other. Neither could get an advantage. After struggling until they were hot and flushed, they eased up but remained watchful.

Tom said, "My big brother can thrash you with his little finger, and I'll make him do it, too."

"I've got a brother that's bigger than yours. He can throw yours over that fence."

Both brothers were imaginary.

With his big toe, Tom drew a line in the dust. "I dare you to step over that. If you do, I'll lick you 'til you can't stand up."

The boy promptly stepped over the line. "Let's see you do it."

"For two cents I *will*."

The boy took two pennies from his pocket and mockingly held them out.

Tom struck them to the ground.

Instantly the boys gripped each other and were tumbling in the dirt. They tugged and tore at each other's hair and clothes, punched and scratched each other's nose, and covered themselves with dust and glory. Tom soon sat astride the new boy, pounding him with his fists. "Holler 'nough," Tom said.

The boy struggled to free himself. He was crying, mainly from rage.

"Holler 'nough." The pounding continued.

At last the stranger got out a smothered "'Nough."

Tom let him up. "That'll learn you. Better look out who you're fooling with next time."

Brushing the dust from his clothes and sniffling, the new boy left, occasionally looking back and threatening what he would do to Tom the next time he encountered him.

Tom jeered, turned his back, and started off, feeling good.

The new boy threw a stone, which hit Tom between the shoulders. Then he ran away.

Tom chased the boy home and took up a position at his front gate, daring the enemy to come out. The enemy only made faces through the window. At last the enemy's mother appeared; called

Tom a vicious, vulgar child; and ordered him away. Tom left, but not without saying that he'd get back at the boy.

Tom got home pretty late that night. He cautiously climbed in through the window. But Aunt Polly was waiting in ambush. When she saw the condition of his clothes, her resolution to turn Tom's Saturday into hard labor became firm.

Chapter 2

Saturday morning the whole summer world was bright, fresh, and brimming with life. There was cheer in every face and a spring in every step. The locust trees were in bloom, and the fragrance of their blossoms filled the air.

Tom appeared on the sidewalk with a bucket of whitewash and a long-handled brush. He examined the board fence. Thirty yards of fence nine feet high. All gladness left him. Life seemed hollow and existence but a burden. Sighing, he dipped his brush and passed it along the top plank, repeated the operation, repeated it again, compared the insignificant whitewashed streak with the far-reaching continent of unwhitewashed fence, and sat down on a tree stump, discouraged.

Carrying a tin pail and singing "Buffalo Gals," Jim came skipping through the gate. Fetching water from the town pump always had been hateful work in Tom's eyes, but now it didn't seem so bad. Tom remembered that there was company at the pump. Children always were there waiting their turn, resting, trading playthings, fighting, and playing. Although the pump was only 150 yards away, Jim never returned with a bucket of water in less than an hour. Even then, somebody usually had to go fetch him.

Tom said, "Say, Jim, I'll fetch the water if you'll do some whitewashing."

Jim shook his head. "Can't, Mas'er Tom. Ol' missis tol' me I got to go an' git dis water an' not fool aroun' wid anybody. She say she expec' Mas'er Tom goin' to ask me to whitewash, so she tol' me to go along an' 'tend to my own business."

"Never mind what she said, Jim. Gimme the bucket. I'll be gone only a minute. She won't ever know."

"I can't, Mas'er Tom. Ol' missis 'ould tear my head off."

"*Her*? She never licks anybody. She just whacks 'em over the head with her thimble. And who cares about that? I'll give you a marble, a crystal clear one."

Jim began to waver.

"Crystal clear, Jim. And it's a big one."

"Dat's a mighty good marble. But I'd better not, Mas'er Tom."

"If you'll whitewash, I'll also show you my sore toe."

Jim was only human. This attraction was too much for him. He put down his pail, took the clear marble, and bent over Tom's toe with keen interest while the bandage was unwound.

In another moment Jim was flying down the street with his pail and a tingling rear, Tom was whitewashing with vigor, and Aunt Polly was retiring from the field with a slipper in her hand and triumph in her eye.

Tom's energy didn't last long. He thought of the fun that he had planned for this day, and his sorrows multiplied. Soon other boys would come tripping along on all sorts of delightful adventures. They would make fun of him for having to work. The very thought burned him like fire. He took out his worldly wealth and examined it: marbles, bits of toys, and trash—enough to buy an exchange of *work* maybe, but not half enough to buy even half an hour of freedom. He returned his meager possessions to his pocket and abandoned the idea of buying other boys' labor. At this hopeless moment he had an inspiration. He took up his brush and calmly went to work.

Ben Rogers soon appeared—the very boy whose ridicule Tom had most dreaded. Ben hopped, skipped, and jumped—proof that his heart was light and his anticipations high. He was eating an apple. At intervals he gave a long, melodious whoop followed by a deep-toned ding dong dong. As he approached, Ben slowed and moved to the middle of the street. He leaned far to the right, then slowly rounded back to the left. He was pretending to be the steamboat *Big Missouri*, as well as captain and engine bells. He imagined himself standing on the hurricane deck giving orders and carrying them out. "Set her back on the starboard! Ting-a-ling-ling." Ben's right hand moved in stately circles representing a forty-foot wheel. "Let her go back on the larboard! Ting-a-ling-ling." Ben's left hand circled.

Tom continued whitewashing, paying no attention to the steamboat.

Ben stared at Tom a moment. "Hey! *You're* up a stump, ain't you?"

No answer. Tom examined his last touch with an artist's eye. He gave his brush another gentle sweep and examined the result, as before.

Ben ranged up alongside him.

Although his mouth watered for Ben's apple, Tom stuck to his work.

"Hello, old chap. You've got to work, huh?"

Tom wheeled sharply around. "Why, it's you, Ben! I hadn't noticed."

"I'm going swimming. Don't you wish *you* could? But of course you'd rather *work*."

Tom briefly contemplated Ben. "What are you calling work?"

"Why, ain't *that* work?"

Tom resumed his whitewashing and answered carelessly. "Maybe it is; maybe it ain't. All I know is, it suits Tom Sawyer."

"Oh, come on. You don't mean to let on that you *like* it."

The brush kept moving. "I don't see why I *shouldn't* like it. Does a boy get a chance to white-wash a fence every day?"

That put the matter in a new light. Ben stopped nibbling his apple.

Tom daintily swept his brush back and forth, stepped back to note the effect, added a touch here and there, and again examined the effect.

Ben watched every move, getting more and more interested. "Say, Tom, let *me* whitewash a little."

Tom considered, was about to consent, then changed his mind. "No. It wouldn't hardly do, Ben. Aunt Polly's awful particular about this fence. It's right here on the street. If it was the back fence, I wouldn't mind, and *she* wouldn't. But she's awful particular about this fence. It's got to be done very careful. I reckon there ain't one boy in a thousand, maybe two thousand, that can do it the way it's got to be done."

"Lemme try. Just a little. I'd let *you* if you was me, Tom."

"I'd like to—honest. But Aunt Polly . . . Well, Jim wanted to do it, and she wouldn't let him. Sid wanted to do it, and she wouldn't let Sid. You see the situation. If you was to tackle this fence and anything was to happen to it . . ."

"Oh, shucks. I'll be careful. Lemme try. Say . . .

I'll give you the core of my apple."

"Well, here. No. I'm afraid . . ."

"I'll give you the whole apple!"

Tom gave up the brush with reluctance in his face but eagerness in his heart.

While the former steamboat worked and sweated in the sun, the retired artist sat nearby on a barrel in the shade, dangled his legs, munched his apple, and planned the slaughter of more innocents. There was no lack of material. Boys happened along every little while. They came to jeer but remained to whitewash. By the time Ben was tired out, Tom had traded the next chance to Billy Fisher for a kite in good repair. When *he* gave out, Johnny Miller bought in for a dead rat and a string to swing it with. And so on and so on, hour after hour.

By mid-afternoon Tom had gone from poverty to wealth. Besides the things already mentioned, he had collected a fragment of chalk, a piece of blue glass to look through, a knife handle, a worn-out window frame, a key that wouldn't unlock anything, the glass stopper from a bottle used to serve wine, a dog collar (but no dog), a brass doorknob, a tin soldier, four pieces of orange peel, six firecrackers, twelve marbles, and a one-eyed kitten. He'd had a good, idle time, with plenty of company, and the fence had received three coats of whitewash. If Tom hadn't run out of whitewash, he would have bankrupted every boy in the town.

Tom told himself that life was not so hollow after all. Without knowing it, he had discovered a law of human psychology: to make someone want something, make that thing hard to get. If Tom had been a great and wise philosopher, like this book's author, he now would have realized that work is whatever someone is *obliged* to do, whereas play is whatever someone is not obliged to do. This would have helped Tom understand why carrying something up a hill is work while mountain climbing is play. He also would have understood that paying to do something makes it play, but *being* paid to do something makes it work.

Tom presented himself before Aunt Polly, who was sitting by an open window. The warm summer air, restful quiet, scent of flowers, and drowsing murmur of the bees had had their effect, and she was nodding over her knitting. She had no company other than her cat, asleep in her lap. Her eyeglasses were propped up on her gray head for safekeeping. She had thought that Tom must have deserted long ago, so she wondered at seeing him place himself in her power in this bold way.

"May I go play now, Aunt?" Tom asked.

"What, already? How much have you done?"

"It's all done."

"Tom, don't lie to me."

"I ain't, Aunt. It *is* all done."

Aunt Polly placed small trust in Tom's statement. She went out to see for herself. When she found the entire fence not only whitewashed but elaborately coated and recoated, her astonishment was great. She said, "Well, I never! You *can* work when you've a mind to." Then she weakened the compliment by adding, "But it's powerful seldom you've a mind to. Well, go 'long and play. But mind you get back some time within a week, or I'll tan you."

She was so overcome by the splendor of his achievement that she took Tom into the closet, selected a choice apple, and gave it to him, along with a lecture on the added value and flavor that a treat has when it comes through virtuous effort. While she closed with a quote from Scripture, Tom grabbed a doughnut.

Then he skipped out. He saw Sid starting up the outside stairway that led to the back rooms on the second floor. Clumps of dirt were handy, and the air was full of them in a twinkling. They raged around Sid like a hailstorm. Before Aunt Polly could collect her surprised faculties and hurry to the rescue, six clumps had hit their mark, and Tom was over the fence and gone. There was a gate, but as a general thing he was too pressed for time to use it. His soul was at peace now that he had settled with Sid for alerting Aunt Polly to the black thread on his shirt.

Tom skirted the block and came around into a muddy alley that passed behind Aunt Polly's cow barn. He got safely beyond capture and punishment and hurried toward the town's public square, where two "military" companies of boys had met for conflict, according to previous appointment. Tom was General of one of these armies; Joe Harper (a bosom friend) was General of the other. These two great commanders did not condescend to fight in person (that being better suited to the smaller fry) but sat together on a hill and conducted the field operations by orders delivered through assistants. Tom's army won a great victory, after a long and hard-fought battle. Then the dead were counted, prisoners exchanged, the terms of the next disagreement agreed on, and the date for the necessary battle set—after which the armies fell into line and marched away. Tom turned homeward alone.

As Tom was passing by the house where Davey Thatcher lived, he saw a new girl in the garden—a lovely little blue-eyed girl with blond hair braided into two long tails, wearing a white dress. The newly crowned hero fell without firing a shot. A certain Amy Lawrence vanished from his heart, leaving no trace. He had thought that he loved Amy to distraction. He had spent months winning her. A week ago, she had confessed to returning his affection. Now he worshipped this new angel. When he saw that she had noticed him, he began to show off in all sorts of absurd ways. By and by, while he was performing some dangerous gymnastics, he glanced aside and saw that the girl was headed toward her house. Tom came up to the fence and leaned on it. The girl halted a moment on the steps and then moved toward the door. Tom heaved a great sigh as she put her foot on the threshold. But his face lit up when she tossed a pansy over the fence a moment before she disappeared.

Tom ran around and stopped within a foot of the flower. He shaded his eyes with his hand and began to look down the street as if he had discovered something interesting going on in that direction. He picked up a straw and tried to balance it on his nose, with his head tilted far back. As he moved from side to side in his efforts, he edged nearer and nearer to the pansy. Finally his bare foot rested on it, his toes closed on it, and he hopped away with the treasure. He disappeared around the corner and buttoned the flower inside his jacket, next to his heart (or his stomach; he was not well informed about anatomy). Then he returned and hung around near the fence until nightfall, showing off as before. But the girl didn't show herself again. Tom comforted himself with the hope that she had been watching him from some window. Finally he reluctantly strode home.

All through supper his spirits were so high that his aunt wondered "what's got into the child." He got a good scolding for having pelted Sid and didn't seem to mind it in the least. He tried to steal sugar under his aunt's very nose and got his knuckles rapped for it.

Tom said, "Aunt, you don't whack Sid when he takes sugar."

"Sid don't torment a body the way you do. You'd always be into that sugar if I wasn't watching you."

Aunt Polly stepped into the kitchen, and Sid reached for the sugar bowl, glorying over Tom. Sid's fingers slipped, and the bowl dropped and broke. Tom was in ecstasy. He decided not to say a word, even when his aunt came in. Instead he would sit perfectly still until she asked who had done the mischief. Then he would tell, and there would be nothing as good in the whole world as to see Sid "catch it."

Aunt Polly returned and stood above the wreckage shooting lightning bolts of anger over her eyeglasses. Tom smugly told himself, "Now it's coming." But the next instant *he* was sprawling on the floor. Aunt Polly's strong palm was raised to strike again when Tom cried out, "Hold on! What are you hitting *me* for? Sid broke it!"

Aunt Polly paused, confused. But when she got her tongue again, she said, "Well, you didn't get a lick you didn't deserve, I reckon. Most likely, you've been into some mischief when I wasn't around." Then her conscience reproached her. She wanted to say something kind and loving, but she judged that discipline forbade that.

Tom sulked in a corner, looking aggrieved. He knew that in her heart his aunt was on her knees to him, and this gratified him. Now and then, a yearning glance fell upon him through a film of tears, but he refused to take notice. He pictured himself brought home from the river, dead, his curls all wet. Aunt Polly would throw herself upon him. Her tears would fall like rain, and she would tell God that, if he would give her back her boy, she never, ever would abuse him again. When his cousin Mary danced in, overjoyed to be home after an age-long visit of one week to the country, he left, in a cloud of self-pity.

Tom sought a desolate place in harmony with his mood. A log raft in the river invited him. He seated himself on its edge and contemplated the river's dreary vastness, wishing that he could drown, instantly. Then he thought of his flower. He took it out, rumpled and wilted. He wondered if *she* would pity him if she knew. Would she cry and wish that she could put her arms around his neck and comfort him? Or would she turn coldly away like the rest of the hollow world? This picture brought such pleasurable suffering that he worked it over again and again in his mind. At last he rose with a sigh and departed in the darkness.

About ten o'clock, he came along the deserted street to where the Adored Unknown lived. He paused a moment. A candle cast a dull glow on the curtain of a second-story window. Was the sacred presence there? He climbed the fence and stole through the plants until he stood under that window. He looked up at it for a long time, with emotion. Then he lay down on the ground under it, on his back, with his hands clasped on his breast and holding his poor wilted flower. Thus he would die. And thus *she* would see him when she looked out in the morning.

The window was raised, a maid's harsh voice broke the holy calm, and a flood of water drenched the poor martyr. The strangling hero sprang up. There was the sound of a missile whizzing through the air, mingled with a murmured curse. The sound of shattering glass followed. Tom shot over the fence and away into the gloom.

Not long after, Tom, undressed for bed, surveyed his drenched garments by candlelight. Sid awoke but said nothing, because there was danger in Tom's eyes. Tom turned in without the added annoyance of prayer, and Sid mentally noted the omission.

Chapter 3

Breakfast over, Aunt Polly held family worship. It began with a prayer built from Scriptural quotations, welded together with a thin mortar of originality. A grim chapter of the Mosaic law followed. Then Tom braced himself and went to work on his verses. Sid had learned *his* days before. Tom turned to memorizing five verses from the Sermon on the Mount—the shortest he could find. After a half hour spent primarily on daydreams, Tom had only a vague idea of his lesson. Mary took his book to hear him recite.

"Blessed are the . . . uh."

"Poor."

"Yes. Poor. Blessed are the poor . . . uh."

"In spirit"

"In spirit. Blessed are the poor in spirit, for they . . ."

"*Theirs.*"

"For *theirs.* Blessed are the poor in spirit, for *theirs* is the kingdom of heaven. Blessed are they that mourn, for they . . . they."

"Sh."

"For they . . ."

"S, H, A."

"For they . . . S, H . . . I don't know what it is!"

"Shall!"

"Oh, *shall!* For they shall . . . mourn. Blessed are they that shall mourn, for they shall . . . Shall *what*? Why don't you tell me, Mary? What do you want to be so mean for?"

"Oh, Tom, you poor thick-headed thing. You must go and learn it again. Don't be discouraged; you'll manage it. And if you do, I'll give you something nice."

"What, Mary?"

"Never you mind. You know that if I say it's nice, it *is* nice."

"Alright, I'll tackle it again."

Under the double pressure of curiosity and potential gain, he recited with shining success. Mary gave him a brand-new knife worth twelve-and-a-half cents. Tom was delighted. True, the knife wouldn't cut anything, but it was fancy, and there was grandeur in that. Tom started to scar the cupboard with it, and was planning to begin on the bureau, when he was called to dress for Sunday school.

Mary gave Tom a basin of water and piece of soap, and he went outside and set the basin on a little bench. He dipped the soap into the water and laid it down, turned up his sleeves, gently poured the water onto the ground, then entered the kitchen and carefully wiped his face on a towel. Mary removed the towel and said, "Now ain't you ashamed, Tom? Water won't hurt you."

Tom was taken aback. The basin was refilled. This time he stood over it awhile, gathering resolution, took a big breath, and began. When he re-entered the kitchen, both eyes shut and groping for the towel, a testimony of suds and water was dripping from his face. But when he emerged from the towel, he wasn't satisfactory because the clean territory stopped at his chin and jaws; below, a dark expanse spread around his neck. Mary took him in hand. When she was done with him, his face lacked the distinction of different colors and his soaked hair was neatly brushed, its short curls shaped into a dainty symmetry. (In private he smoothed out the curls, with considerable labor, and plastered his hair against his head because he considered curls effeminate.)

Mary got out his Sunday suit, which was called his "other clothes" (by that, you know the size of his wardrobe). After Tom had dressed, Mary buttoned his neat shirt up to his chin, turned his vast collar down over his shoulders, brushed him off, and crowned him with his speckled straw hat. He now looked greatly improved and uncomfortable. There was a restraint about cleanliness and whole clothes that galled him. He hoped that

Mary would forget his shoes, but she brought them out and coated them with animal fat. He lost his temper and said that he always was being forced to do things that he didn't want to do. Mary said, "Please, Tom. Be a good boy." So he got into the shoes, snarling. Mary soon was ready, and the three children set out for Sunday school, which Mary and Sid liked and Tom hated.

Sunday school hours were 9:00 to 10:30. Church service followed. Mary and Sid always remained for the sermon voluntarily; Tom always remained for stronger reasons. The church's high-backed, uncushioned pews would seat about three hundred people. The building was small and plain, with a box-like wooden steeple.

At the door Tom dropped back a step and accosted a Sunday-dressed comrade. "Say, Billy, got a yellow ticket?"

"Yes."

"What'll you take for it?"

"What'll you give?"

"Piece of licorice and a fish hook."

"Let's see 'em."

Tom exhibited them.

They were satisfactory, and the property changed hands. Then Tom traded a couple of white marbles for three red tickets, and some trifle for a couple of blue ones. He waylaid other boys as they came, and went on buying tickets of various colors for about ten minutes.

Tom entered the church with a swarm of clean but noisy boys and girls, proceeded to his seat, and started a quarrel with the first boy who was handy. The teacher, a grave, elderly man, interfered, then turned his back a moment. Tom pulled the hair of a boy in the next bench and appeared to be absorbed in his book when the boy turned around. Tom stuck a pin in another boy, to hear him say "Ouch!" and got a new rebuke from the teacher.

Tom's class members all were alike: restless, noisy, and troublesome. When the time came for them to recite their lessons, not one of them knew his verses perfectly. All had to be prompted. However, they struggled through.

For every two verses that they recited, each student got a small blue ticket with a Scriptural passage on it. Ten blue tickets could be exchanged for one red ticket, ten red tickets could be exchanged for one yellow, and for ten yellow tickets a pupil received a Bible worth forty cents. How many of my readers would have the industry to memorize two thousand verses, even for the fanciest Bible? Yet, through two years of patient work, Mary had acquired two Bibles this way. Billy Richter had earned four or five. He once recited three thousand verses without stopping. But the strain on his brain was too great; from that day on, he barely was smarter than an idiot. Only the older pupils managed to keep their tickets and stick to their tedious work long enough to receive a

Bible—presented, in a public ceremony, by the superintendent—so the delivery of one of these prizes was rare and noteworthy. For one day, the successful pupil was so great and celebrated that all other students felt fresh ambition, which often lasted a couple of weeks. Tom's mind never hungered for a Bible, but it did hunger for the glory that came with it.

In due course the superintendent, Henry Walters, stood in front of the pulpit, with a closed hymn book in his hand and his forefinger inserted between its pages, and commanded attention. When a Sunday-school superintendent makes their customary little speech, a hymn book in the hand is as necessary as a sheet of music in the hand of a solo singer—although *why* is a mystery; neither the superintendent nor the singer ever refers to what they're holding. This superintendent was a slim man of thirty-five, with a sandy goatee and short sandy hair. He wore a stiff standing collar whose upper edge almost reached his ears and whose sharp points curved forward near the corners of his mouth. The collar was a fence that compelled him to look straight ahead and turn his whole body when a side view was required. His chin was propped on a spreading cravat as broad and long as a dollar bill, with fringed ends. The toes of his boots turned sharply up, like a sleigh's runners—an effect that young men patiently and laboriously produced by sitting with their toes pressed against a wall for hours at a time. Walters was very earnest; he held sacred things in such reverence that his Sunday-school voice had an intonation wholly absent on weekdays.

He began, "Now, children, I want you all to sit up as straight as you can and give me your full attention for a minute or two. That's it. That's the way good little boys and girls should behave. I see one little girl who is looking out of the window; I'm afraid she thinks I am out there somewhere, perhaps up in one of the trees making a speech to the little birds. [Appreciative laughter.] I want to tell you how good it makes me feel to see so many bright, clean little faces assembled in a place like this, learning to do right and be good." And so forth and so on.

The last part of Walters' speech was marred by fighting and other recreations among some of the boys, and by widespread fidgetings and whisperings that washed even to the bases of isolated, incorruptible rocks like Mary and Sid. The conclusion of Walters' speech was received with a burst of silent gratitude.

Much of the whispering had been caused by the entrance of visitors: Jeff Thatcher, one of the town's lawyers; a very feeble, aged man; a heavyset, middle-aged gentleman with iron-gray hair; and a dignified lady who was surely the heavyset gentleman's wife. The lady was leading a child. Tom had been restless and conscience-smitten (he could not bring himself to meet Amy Lawrence's loving gaze); but when he saw this small newcomer, his soul was ablaze with bliss. The next moment he was showing off with all his might: cuffing boys, pulling hair, making faces, using every art that seemed likely to fascinate a girl and win her applause.

The visitors were given seats of honor. As soon as Walters finished his speech, he introduced them to the school. The middle-aged man turned out to be a county judge, the grandest person these children ever had looked upon. And he was from Constantinople, a whole twelve miles away, so he had traveled and seen the world. His eyes had looked upon the county courthouse, which was said to have a tin roof. This was the great Judge Thatcher, Jeff Thatcher's brother.

Walters fell to showing off—giving orders, delivering judgments, and discharging directions. The librarian, too, showed off—running hither and thither, his arms full of books, with all of the fuss that insect authority delights in. The women teachers showed off by bending sweetly over pupils whom they previously boxed, lifting warning fingers at bad little boys, and lovingly patting good ones. The men teachers showed off with scoldings and other displays of authority. Most of the teachers, of both sexes, found that they needed to do things up at the library, by the pulpit—needed to do them two or three times. The little girls showed off in various ways, and the little boys showed off with such diligence that the air was thick with paper wads and scufflings.

Judge Thatcher sat and beamed a majestic judicial smile on everyone present, warming himself in the sun of his own grandeur.

Walters needed only one more thing to make his ecstasy complete: a chance to deliver a Bible prize. Several pupils had a few yellow tickets, but none had enough. He would have given worlds to have Billy Richter back with a sound mind. At this moment, when hope was dead, Tom Sawyer came forward with nine yellow tickets, nine red ones, and ten blue ones, and demanded a Bible. This was a thunderbolt out of a clear sky. Walters never had expected to give a Bible to *this* pupil. But there was no getting around it. Therefore, Tom was elevated to a place with the Judge and the other visitors, and Walters announced the great news. It was the most stunning surprise of the decade. The other boys were consumed with envy. Those who had traded tickets to Tom suffered the bitterest pangs. Walters bestowed the prize with as much gushing as he could manage under the circumstances. The poor fellow knew that there was some mystery here that could not bear the light.

Amy Lawrence was proud and glad, and she tried to make Tom see it in her face, but he wouldn't look at her. She started to suspect, and a glance that followed Tom's eyes to the new girl told her worlds. Tears came, and she hated everyone—Tom most of all (she thought).

Tom was introduced to the Judge, but he couldn't speak and scarcely could breathe, partly because of the Judge's awful greatness, partly because the Judge was *her* father. The Judge put his hand on Tom's head, called Tom a fine little man, and asked him what his name was.

Tom stammered, "Tom. No. Thomas."

"That's it. But you've another name, I daresay."

"Tell the gentleman your other name, Thomas," Walters said. "And say *sir*."

"Thomas Sawyer, sir."

"That's a good boy. Two thousand verses is a great many. You never will be sorry for the trouble you took to learn them. Someday you'll be a great and good man, Thomas. Then you'll look back and say, 'It's all owing to the precious Sunday-school privileges of my boyhood, to my dear teachers, and to the good superintendent who encouraged me and gave me a beautiful Bible.' That is what you will say, Thomas. Now, tell me and this lady some of the things you've learned. No doubt, you know the names of the twelve disciples. Tell us the names of the first two."

Tom tugged at a buttonhole. He blushed, and his eyes fell. Walters thought, "The boy can't answer the simplest question. Why *did* the Judge ask him?" Yet Walters felt obliged to say, "Answer the gentleman, Thomas. Don't be afraid." Tom remained silent. "I know you'll tell me," the lady said.

"The names of the first two disciples were . . . David and Goliath!"

Let us charitably draw a curtain over the rest of the scene.

Chapter 4

About 10:30, the church's cracked bell began to ring, and people gathered for the morning sermon. The Sunday-school children occupied pews with their parents. Tom, Sid, and Mary sat with Aunt Polly. Tom was placed on the aisle, as far as possible from the open window and seductive outdoor summer scenes. The crowd filed up the aisles: the aged and needy postmaster; the mayor and his wife (the town had a mayor, among other unnecessaries); the justice of the peace; Caroline Douglas, a smart, wealthy, and generous widow of forty (her hill mansion was the town's only palace); the bent and venerable Major and Mrs. Ward; lawyer Riverson; the town beauty, followed by other ribbon-decked heart-breakers; all the young clerks in town (a circling wall of oiled and simpering admirers, they had stood in the entry hall until the last young woman had passed); and, lastly, Willie Mufferson, the Model Boy, taking as much heedful care of his mother as if she were glass. He always brought his mother to church and was the pride of all the matrons. The boys all hated him because he was so good and so often held up to them as a model. Willie had a white handkerchief. Tom considered any boy with a handkerchief a snob.

The bell rang once more—a call to any stragglers. Then a solemn hush fell on the assembly; it was broken only by the tittering and whispering of the choir in the gallery. The choir always tittered and whispered throughout the service. There once was a well-behaved church choir, but I have forgotten where it was—in some foreign country, I think.

The minister, Reverend Sprague, read the hymn with enthusiasm. He was considered a wonderful reader. At church gatherings he always was asked to read poetry. When he finished, the ladies would cover their eyes and shake their head as if to say, "Words cannot express how beautiful it is, too beautiful for this earth." After the hymn Reverend Sprague read notices of meetings. It seemed the list would stretch to Doomsday. Then he prayed. He pleaded for the church, the church's little children, the town's other churches, the town itself, the county, the state, the United States, the churches of the United States, Congress, the President, sailors tossed by stormy seas, the millions oppressed by European monarchs or Oriental despots, and the heathens in far-off islands. He closed with a plea that his words might find favor and be as seed sown in fertile ground, yielding in time a harvest of good. Amen.

Dresses rustled, and the standing congregation sat down. Tom did not enjoy the prayer; he only endured it. Whenever Reverend Sprague added something new, Tom resented it; he considered additions unfair. In the midst of the prayer, a fly had lit on the back of the pew in front of him. The fly tortured Tom's spirit by rubbing her hands together, embracing her head with her arms and polishing it vigorously, scraping her wings with her hind legs and smoothing them to her body—going through her entire toilet with the utmost calm. Tom itched to grab the fly, but he didn't dare; he believed that his soul would be instantly destroyed if he did such a thing during prayer. But the instant after "Amen," the fly was his prisoner. His aunt detected the act and made Tom let her go.

Reverend Sprague read his sermon, droning through an argument so wordy that many a head began to nod. It was an argument that dealt in limitless fire and brimstone and thinned the predestined elect down to so few as to hardly be worth saving. Tom counted the sermon's pages. After church he always knew how many pages the sermon had been, but he seldom knew anything else about it. However, this time he actually was interested for a little while. Reverend Sprague spoke of the millennium, when a lion and lamb would lie down together and a child would lead the world's people. The moral was lost on Tom, who thought only of the principal character's conspicuousness before onlooking nations. He wished that he could be that child, if the lion was tame. As the dry argument resumed, Tom lapsed once more into suffering. It was a genuine relief to the whole congregation when the ordeal was over and the benediction pronounced.

Chapter 5

Monday morning found Tom miserable, as every Monday morning did. It began another week's slow suffering in school. Tom generally began Mondays wishing that he had not enjoyed a holiday; holidays just made returning to captivity more unbearable.

Tom lay thinking. If he were sick, he could stay home from school. He checked his system but found no ailment. Then he discovered that one of his upper front teeth was loose. He was about to start groaning when it occurred to him that if he went to his aunt saying he had a loose tooth, she simply would pull it out, and that would hurt. So he decided to hold the tooth in reserve. After a while he remembered that he had a sore toe, so he started groaning. Sid slept on. Tom groaned louder. No reaction from Sid. Tom gave a series of admirable groans. Sid snored on. Tom was aggravated. "Sid! Sid!" He shook Sid. This worked. Tom resumed his groaning. Sid yawned, stretched, brought himself up on his elbow, and stared at Tom, who kept groaning.

"Tom. Say, Tom!"

No response.

"Tom! What's the matter?" Sid shook Tom and looked into his face anxiously.

Tom moaned, "Don't, Sid. Don't joggle me."

"Why? What's the matter? I'll call Auntie."

"No. It'll be over soon, maybe. Don't call anybody."

"I have to. How long have you been like this?"

"Hours. Ouch! Don't stir so much, Sid. You'll kill me."

"Why didn't you wake me sooner? What *is* the matter?"

"I forgive you everything, Sid [groan]—everything you've ever done to me. When I'm gone . . ."

"Oh, Tom, you ain't dying, are you? Maybe . . ."

"Give my one-eyed cat to the new girl that's come to town. Tell her . . ."

But Sid had snatched his clothes and gone. He flew downstairs. "Aunt Polly, come! Tom's dying!"

"Dying!"

"Yes. Come quick!"

"Rubbish! I don't believe it." But she hurried upstairs, with Sid and Mary at her heels. When she reached the bed, she cried, "Tom, what's the matter with you?"

"Oh, Auntie, I'm . . ."

"What's the matter with you?"

"My sore toe!"

Aunt Polly sank into a chair and laughed a little, cried a little, and did both together a little. This restored her. "Tom, what a turn you gave me. Now you stop this nonsense."

The groans ceased. "Aunt Polly, it hurt so much that I didn't mind my tooth."

"Your tooth, indeed! What's the matter with your tooth?"

"It's loose, and it aches awful."

"Don't begin that groaning again. Open your mouth. Well, your tooth *is* loose, but you're not going to die from it. Mary, get me some thread and a hot chunk from the fire."

"Oh, please don't pull it out, Auntie," Tom said. "It don't hurt any more. I swear it don't. Please don't, Auntie. I don't want to have to stay home from school."

"Oh, you don't, don't you? So all this row was because you thought you'd get to stay home from school and go fishing? Tom, you seem to try every way you can to break my old heart."

The dental instruments were ready. Aunt Polly fastened one end of the thread to Tom's tooth and the other to the bedpost. Then she seized the fiery chunk and thrust it almost into Tom's face. The tooth hung dangling by the bedpost.

But all trials bring compensations. As Tom headed to school after breakfast, he was the envy of every boy he met because the gap in his teeth enabled him to spit in a new and admirable way. He gathered quite a following of lads interested in the exhibition.

Tom soon encountered the town's young outcast, Huckleberry Finn, son of the town drunkard. Huckleberry was hated by all the mothers of the town because he was idle, lawless, vulgar, and bad and because their children admired him, delighted in his forbidden society, and wished they dared to be like him. Like the other boys, Tom was under strict orders not to play with Huckleberry. So he played with him every chance he got. Huckleberry always was dressed in men's cast-off rags. His hat was a ruin with a wide crescent lopped out of its brim. His coat, when he wore one, hung nearly to his heels. Only one suspender supported his trousers, whose seat bagged low and whose fringed legs dragged in the dirt when they weren't rolled up.

Huckleberry came and went as he chose. He slept on doorsteps in fine weather and in empty barrels in wet weather. He didn't have to go to school or church or obey anyone. He could go fishing or swimming when and where he chose, and stay as long as he liked. No one forbade him to fight. He could stay up as late as he pleased. He always was the first boy to go barefoot in the spring and the last to wear shoes in the fall. He never had to wash or put on clean clothes. He could swear wonderfully. In a word, he had everything that makes life precious. So thought every harassed, hampered, respectable boy in St. Petersburg.

Tom hailed the romantic outcast, "Hello, Huck!"

"Hello."

"What's that you've got?"

"Dead cat."

"Lemme see. He's pretty stiff. Where'd you get him?"

"Bought him off a boy."

"What did you give?"

"A blue ticket and a bladder that I got at the slaughterhouse."

"Where'd you get the blue ticket?"

"Bought it off Ben Rogers two weeks ago."

"What is dead cats good for?"

"Cure warts with."

"Really? I know something that's better."

"What?"

"Stump water," Tom said.

"Stump water! I wouldn't give a darn for stump water."

"Did you ever try it?"

"No, but Bob Tanner did."

"Who told you so?"

"Bob told Davey Thatcher, and Davey told Johnny Baker, and Johnny told Jim Hollis, and Jim told Ben Rogers, and Ben told me."

"Well, what of it? They'll all lie. Tell me how Bob Tanner done it," Tom said.

"He dipped his hand in a rotten stump where

the rainwater was."

"In the daytime?"

"Yes."

"With his face to the stump?"

"Yes. At least, I reckon so."

"Did he say anything?"

"I don't know."

"Aha! You can't cure warts with stump water in such a fool way. You've got to go, alone, into the woods, where there's a stump with rainwater. Right at midnight, you back up against the stump, jam your hand in, and say, 'Barley corn, barley corn, spells of all sorts. Stump water, stump water, swaller these warts,' and then walk away quick, eleven steps, with your eyes shut, and then turn around three times and walk home without speaking to anybody. If you speak, the charm's busted."

"Well, that sounds like a good way, but that ain't the way Bob Tanner done it."

"You can bet he didn't, 'cause he's the wartiest boy in this town. He wouldn't have a wart on him if he'd knowed how to work stump water. I've took thousands of warts off my hands that way. But say, how do you cure 'em with dead cats?"

"Why, you take your cat and go to the grave-yard after somebody wicked has been buried. You go about midnight, when a devil will come—or maybe two or three. You can't see 'em; you only can hear something like the wind or maybe hear 'em talk. When the devils are taking the wicked person away, you heave your cat at 'em and say, 'Devil follow corpse; cat follow devil; warts follow cat; I'm done with ye.' That'll fetch any wart."

"Sounds right. Did you ever try it?"

"No, but old Mother Hopkins told me."

"Well, I reckon it's so, then, 'cause they say she's a witch."

"I *know* she is. She witched pap. Pap says so his own self. He come along one day, and he seen she was a-witchin' him, so he took up a rock. If she hadn't dodged, he would've got her. That very night he rolled off a shed where he was layin' drunk and broke his arm."

"How did he know she was a-witchin' him?"

"Pap can tell. Pap says when they keep lookin' right at you, they're a-witchin' you, 'specially if they mumble, 'cause when they mumble, they're saying the Lord's Prayer backwards."

"Say, Huck, when you goin' to try the cat?"

"Tonight. I reckon devils'll come after old Hoss Williams tonight."

"But they buried him Saturday. Didn't the devils get him Saturday night?"

"How you talk! How could their charms work before midnight? And *then* it's Sunday. Devils don't hang around much on a Sunday, I reckon."

"That's so. Can I go with you?"

"Of course, if you ain't afeard."

"Afeard? Ain't likely. Will you meow?"

"Yes, and you meow back if you get a chance.

Last time you kep' me meowin' 'til old Hays went to throwin' rocks at me, sayin' 'Dern that cat!' I threw a brick through his window. Don't tell."

"I won't. I couldn't meow that night 'cause Auntie was watching me, but I'll meow this time."

The boys parted, and Tom continued on his way. When he reached the little schoolhouse, he strode in, hung his hat on a peg, and flung himself into his seat. Enthroned in his great armchair, the schoolmaster, Silas Dobbins, was dozing. The interruption roused him. "Thomas Sawyer!"

Tom knew that hearing his full name meant trouble. "Sir."

"Come up here. Why are you late again?"

Tom was about to lie when he saw two long tails of blond hair hanging down a back that he recognized by the electric sympathy of love. Next to that form was the only vacant place on the girls' side of the schoolhouse. Tom instantly said, "I stopped to talk with Huckleberry Finn."

Dobbins' pulse stopped, and he stared. The buzz of study ceased. The pupils wondered if this foolhardy boy had lost his mind. Dobbins asked, "You did what?"

"Stopped to talk with Huckleberry Finn."

"Thomas Sawyer, this is the most astounding confession I ever have heard. Take off your jacket."

Dobbins hit Tom with switches until his arm was tired and his supply of switches was noticeably diminished. "Now, sir, go and sit with the *girls*!

And let this be a warning to you."

Titters rippled around the room, but Tom sat down next to his idol. The girl looked away with a toss of her head. Nudges, winks, and whispers traveled the room. Tom sat still, with his arms on the long, low desk before him, and seemed to study his book. The usual murmur of students soon resumed, and Tom began to steal glances at the girl. She noticed his glances, made a face at him, and gave him the back of her head. When she cautiously faced around again, a peach lay before her. She thrust it away. Tom gently put it back. She thrust it away again but with less hostility. Tom patiently returned it to its place. She let it remain.

Tom scrawled on his slate, "Please take it; I got more." The girl glanced at the words but made no sign. Tom began to draw on the slate, hiding his work with his left hand. For a time the girl refused to notice, but then she whispered, "Let me see it." Tom partly uncovered a dismal caricature of a house with a corkscrew of smoke issuing from the chimney. The girl's interest fastened onto the work. When it was finished, the girl gazed a moment, then whispered, "It's nice. Draw a man." The artist erected a man in the front yard who looked like an oil tower. He could have stepped over the house, but the girl was not hypercritical. She whispered, "It's a beautiful man. I wish I could draw."

"It's easy," Tom whispered. "I'll learn you."

"Oh, will you? When?"

"At noon. Do you go home for lunch?"

"I'll stay if you will."

"Good. What's your name?"

"Becky Thatcher. What's yours? Oh, I know. It's Thomas Sawyer."

"That's the name they lick me by. I'm Tom when I'm good. Call me Tom, alright?"

"Yes."

Tom began to scrawl on the slate, hiding the words from Becky. She begged to see. Tom said, "Oh, it ain't anything."

"Please let me see." Becky put her small hand on his, and a little scuffle followed, with Tom pretending to resist but letting his hand slip until these words were revealed: "I love you."

"Oh, you bad thing!" She gave his hand a smart rap but reddened and looked pleased.

Just then Tom was gripped and lifted by his ear. In that vise he was borne across the room and deposited in his own seat, under a barrage of student giggles. Dobbins stood over him a few awful moments, then returned to his throne without a word. Although Tom's ear tingled, Tom's heart rejoiced. As the students quieted, Tom made an honest effort to study, but the turmoil within him was too great. When his turn came to read, he botched the job. In geography class he turned lakes into mountains, mountains into rivers, and rivers into continents. In spelling class he missed baby words and was forced to relinquish the pewter spelling medal that he had worn, conspicuously, for months.

When school broke up at noon, Tom flew to Becky and whispered into her ear, "Put on your bonnet, and let on you're going home. When you get to the corner, give the rest of 'em the slip. Turn down through the lane, and come back. I'll go the other way." So Becky went off with one group of students, and Tom with another. In a little while the two met at the bottom of the lane. When they reached the school, they had it all to themselves. They sat together, with a slate before them, and Tom gave Becky the pencil and held her hand in his, guiding it, and so created another house. When the interest in art began to wane, the two fell to talking.

"Do you like rats?" Tom asked.

"No!"

"I mean dead ones, to swing around your head with a string."

"No. What *I* like is chewing gum."

"I should say so! I wish I had some now."

"I've got some. I'll let you chew it awhile, but you must give it back to me."

That was agreeable, so they took turns chewing it and dangled their legs against the bench in an excess of contentment.

"Was you ever at a circus?" Tom asked.

"Yes, and my pa's going to take me again some time if I'm good."

"I been to the circus three or four times. Church ain't shucks to a circus. When I grow up, I'm going to be a circus clown."

"Are you? That will be nice. They're lovely."

"Yes. And they get loads of money—almost a dollar a day, Ben Rogers says. Say, Becky, was you ever engaged?"

"What's that?"

"Engaged to be married."

"No."

"Would you like to be?"

"I don't know. What's it like?"

"Why, it ain't like anything. You just tell a boy you won't ever have anybody but him. Then you kiss, and that's all. Anybody can do it."

"What do you kiss for?"

"Why, that's to . . . Well, they always do that."

"Everybody?"

"Yes, everybody that's in love with each other. Do you remember what I wrote on the slate? I'll whisper it."

Becky hesitated, but Tom took silence for consent. He put his arm around her waist and whispered with his mouth close to her ear. "Now you whisper it to me."

She resisted awhile, then said, "Turn your face away so you can't see. You mustn't ever tell anybody. You won't, will you?"

"No, indeed."

Tom turned his face away. Becky bent timidly

around until her breath stirred his curls and whispered, "I love you." Then she sprang away and ran around and around the desks and benches, with Tom after her. At last she took refuge in a corner, with her little white apron to her face.

Tom clasped her around her neck and said, "It's all done now, Becky, except for the kiss. Don't be afraid of that. It ain't anything at all. Please, Becky." He tugged at her apron and hands.

Her hands dropped. Her face, glowing with the struggle, came up and submitted.

Tom kissed her red lips. "Now it's all done, Becky. After this, you ain't ever to love or marry anybody but me, never ever."

"I'll never love or marry anybody but you, Tom. And you ain't ever to marry anybody but me."

"Of course. That's part of it. And whenever we come to school or go home, you're to walk with me, when there ain't anybody looking. And you choose me and I choose you at parties because that's what you do when you're engaged."

"It's nice. I never heard of it before."

"It's ever so gay! Why, me and Amy Lawrence . . ."

Becky's big eyes told Tom his blunder. "Oh, Tom! I ain't the first girl you've been engaged to!" Becky began to cry.

"Don't cry, Becky. I don't care for her anymore." Tom tried to put his arm around her neck, but she pushed him away and turned her face to the wall. Tom tried again, with soothing words, and again was rejected. Then his pride was up. He strode away and went outside.

Tom stood awhile, restless and uneasy, periodically glancing at the door, hoping that Becky would repent and come to find him. She didn't. Then he began to fear that he was in the wrong, so he went back in. Becky still was standing in the corner, with her face to the wall. Tom went to her and stood a moment, not knowing how to proceed. "Becky, I . . . I don't care for anybody but you."

No reply.

"Becky, won't you say something?"

No.

Tom got out his most prized possession, a brass knob from the top of an andiron, and passed it around her so that she could see it. "Please, Becky. Won't you take it?"

Becky knocked it to the floor.

Tom marched out.

Becky soon ran to the door and around the playground. Tom wasn't in sight. She called, "Tom! Tom!" No answer. When the other pupils returned minus Tom, Becky ached with regret.

Chapter 6

Tom dodged hither and thither through lanes until he was well out of the path of returning students. Half an hour later he was behind the Douglas mansion on Cardiff Hill, and the schoolhouse was hardly visible in the valley behind him. He entered a dense wood, picked his way to its center, and sat down under a spreading oak. No breeze stirred. The noonday heat had even stilled the song of birds. Nature lay in a trance broken only by the occasional far-off hammering of a woodpecker. Tom was steeped in melancholy. He sat with his elbows on his knees and his chin in his hands. If only he had a clean Sunday-school record, he'd be willing to die, he thought. As for Becky—what had he done? Nothing. She'd be sorry someday, maybe when it was too late. If only he could die *temporarily*.

The idea of being a clown returned to him, but frivolity, jokes, and spotted tights now seemed entirely too merry. No, he would be a pirate. His name would spread throughout the world, making people shudder. He would plow the sea in a black-hulled ship flying a skull-and-crossbones flag. At the height of his fame, he would return to his hometown. He would enter the church, tanned and weather-beaten, in a black velvet outfit with a crimson sash, a belt bristling with pistols, a crime-rusted sword at his side, and a big floppy hat with waving plumes. The congregation would whisper, "It's Tom Sawyer, the pirate—the black avenger!" Yes, he would run away from home and become a pirate. He'd start the very next morning. He must get ready and gather his resources.

Tom went to a nearby rotten log and began to dig under one end with his knife. He soon struck wood that sounded hollow. He put his hand there and uttered this incantation: "What isn't here, *come*. What *is* here, *stay*." He scraped away the dirt, exposing a little treasure-box made of shingles. In it lay a marble. Tom was astonished. "Well, that beats anything." He tossed the marble away and stood thinking. A superstition of his had failed. He and his comrades had believed that if you bury a marble with certain incantations, leave it for two weeks, and then dig it up, you'll find all the marbles that you ever lost. He decided that some witch had interfered and broken the charm.

The blast of a toy trumpet now sounded faintly through the forest. Tom flung off his jacket and trousers, turned a suspender into a belt, and raked away some brush behind the rotten log, revealing a crude bow and arrow, a wooden sword, and a tin trumpet. He seized these things and bounded away, barelegged, his shirt fluttering. Tom halted under a large elm, blew an answering blast, and began to tiptoe and look around cautiously. He told an imaginary company, "Hold, my merry men. Keep hid 'til I blow."

Tom's friend Joe Harper now appeared, as airily clad and elaborately armed as Tom.

Tom called, "Hold! Who comes here into Sherwood Forest without my pass?"

"Guy of Guisborne needs no man's pass. Who art thou that . . . that?"

"Dares to speak such language," Tom prompted (because they spoke from memory).

"Who art thou that dares to speak such language?"

"I am Robin Hood, as thy slain body soon shall know."

"Art thou that famous outlaw? Right gladly will I have at thee."

They took their wooden swords, dumped their other trappings on the ground, struck a fencing pose, and began a grave combat. By and by, Tom shouted, "Fall! Why don't you fall?"

"I won't. Why don't *you* fall? You're getting the worst of it."

"I can't fall. That ain't the way it is in the book. The book says, 'Then with one backhanded stroke, he slew Guy of Guisborne.' You're supposed to turn around and let me hit you in the back."

There was no getting around the authorities, so Joe turned, received the whack, and fell.

After carrying out more adventures of the same sort, Tom and Joe dressed themselves, hid their trappings, and went off grieving that there were no outlaws anymore. They thought that they would rather be outlaws for a year than President of the United States forever.

Chapter 7

At 9:30 that night, Tom and Sid were sent to bed, as usual. They said their prayers, and Sid soon was asleep. Tom lay awake in restless impatience. When it seemed to him that it must be nearly daylight, he heard the clock strike ten. Only ten! Tom soon dozed off, in spite of himself. The clock chimed eleven, but he didn't hear it. Then the raising of a nearby window disturbed him. A cry of "Scat, you devil!" and the crash of an empty bottle against his aunt's woodshed brought him wide awake. A minute later he was dressed, out the window, and creeping along the roof on all fours. He cautiously meowed once or twice, then jumped to the woodshed's roof and then to the ground. Huck was there with his dead cat.

The boys set off into the gloom. A half hour later they were wading through the graveyard's tall grass. The graveyard was on a hill, about a mile and a half from the town. Around it was a board fence that leaned inward in some places, leaned outward in others, and stood upright nowhere. Grass and weeds grew wild over the whole cemetery. All the old graves were sunken in. There was not a tombstone in the place. Round-topped, worm-eaten boards leaned over the graves. "Sacred to the memory of So-and-So" had once been painted on them, but the inscriptions no longer were visible.

A faint wind moaned through the trees. Tom feared it might be the spirits of the dead, complaining about being disturbed. The boys talked little, and only under their breath, because the time, place, and solemnity oppressed their spirits. They found the new grave they were seeking and hid themselves among three large elms that grew within a few feet of it. The hooting of a distant owl was the only sound that broke the stillness.

Tom whispered, "Huck, do you think that the dead people mind us being here?"

"I wish I knowed," Huck whispered back, "It's awful solemn-like, ain't it?" There was a long pause while the boys considered this matter. "Do you reckon that Hoss Williams hears us talking?" Huck said.

"Course he does. At least, his spirit does."

"I wish I'd said *Mister* Williams. I didn't mean any harm. Everybody calls him Hoss."

Suddenly Tom seized Huck's arm. "Sh!"

"What is it?" The two clung together.

"There it is again. Didn't you hear it?"

"Lord, Tom, spirits are coming! They're coming

for sure. What'll we do?"

"I don' know. Think they'll see us?"

"They can see in the dark, same as cats."

The boys bent their heads together and scarcely breathed. A muffled sound of voices floated up from the graveyard's far end.

"Look!" Tom whispered. Some vague figures approached through the gloom, swinging a tin lantern that freckled the ground with light.

"It's devils," Huck whispered with a shudder. "Three of 'em. Lordy, Tom, we're goners. Can you pray?"

"I'll try. 'Now I lay me down to . . .'"

"They're humans!" Huck interrupted. "One of 'em's old Muff Potter. *He* ain't sharp enough to notice us. Drunk, most likely."

"I know another o' them voices. It's Injun Joe."

"That murderin' half-breed! I'd rather they was devils."

The whispers died out now because the three men had reached the grave and stood within a few feet of the boys' hiding place.

"Here it is," the third man said. He held up a lantern. Its light revealed the face of young Dr. Robinson.

Potter and Joe carried a wheelbarrow with a rope and a couple of shovels on it. They dropped their load and began to open the grave. Robinson put the lantern at the head of the grave and sat down with his back against one of the elm trees.

He was so close that the boys could have touched him. "Hurry, men," he said in a low voice. "The moon might come out at any moment."

The others growled a response and went on digging. For some time there was no noise except the grating of the shovels discharging their freight of dirt and gravel. Finally a shovel struck the coffin. The men quickly hoisted the coffin and, with their shovels, pried off its lid. They removed the body and dumped it onto the ground. The moon drifted from behind the clouds and lit the corpse's pale face. The three men placed the corpse on the wheelbarrow, covered it with a blanket, and bound it in place with rope. Potter took out a large knife and cut off the rope's dangling end. Then he said, "Now the cussed thing's ready, Robinson. You'll out with another five, or here it stays."

"What do you mean?" Robinson said. "I've paid you already."

"Yes, and you done more than that," Joe said, approaching Robinson, who was standing now. "One night five years ago you drove me away from your father's kitchen when I came to ask for something to eat. When I swore I'd get even with you if it took a hundred years, your father had me jailed for vagrancy. Did you think I'd forget? Now I've *got* you, and you've got to settle." His fist was in Robinson's face.

Robinson struck Joe, knocking him to the ground. Potter dropped his knife and exclaimed,

"Don't you hit my pardner!" The next moment he and Robinson were grappling with each other. Joe sprang to his feet, his eyes aflame, and snatched up Potter's knife. He circled the combatants, waiting for the right opportunity. Robinson flung himself free, seized the heavy headboard of Williams' grave, and felled Potter with it. In the same instant, Joe drove the knife into Robinson's chest. Robinson reeled and fell partly on Potter, flooding him with his blood. The clouds blotted out the dreadful spectacle, and the two frightened boys fled in the dark.

When the moon reemerged, Joe stood contemplating the two forms. Robinson murmured indistinctly, gasped, and was still. Joe muttered, "*That* score is settled. Damn you." Then he robbed the body. He placed the fatal knife in Potter's open right hand and sat down on the dismantled coffin. Several minutes passed. Then Potter began to stir and moan. His hand closed on the knife; he raised it, glanced at it, and let it fall, with a shudder. Potter sat up, pushing Robinson's body from him. Confusedly he gazed at the body and his surroundings. His eyes met Joe's. "Lord, what's this, Joe?"

"It's a dirty business," Joe said without moving.

"Why'd you do it?"

"I didn't do it."

Potter trembled and went white. "I shouldn't 've drunk tonight. I thought I'd gotten sober. I can't recollect anything, hardly. Tell me, Joe—honest now. Did I do it? I never meant to, 'pon my soul. It's awful, and him so young and promising."

"You two was scuffling. He hit you with the headboard, and you fell flat. You staggered up, snatched the knife, and jammed it into him just as he hit you again. And here you've laid, dead as a post, 'til now."

"I didn't know what I was doing. I wish I may die this minute if I did. It was all on account of the whiskey and the excitement, I reckon. I never used a weapon in my life before. Joe, don't tell! Say you won't tell. I always liked you and stood up for you. You won't tell, will you?"

"You've always been fair and square with me, Muff Potter, and I won't go back on you. I won't tell."

"Bless you for this, Joe." Potter began to cry.

"This ain't any time for blubbering. Be off, and don't leave any tracks."

Potter started on a trot that quickly increased to a run. Joe stood looking after him. A few minutes later the murdered man, blanketed corpse, lidless coffin, and open grave were under no inspection but the moon's.

Tom and Huck flew toward the town. From time to time, they glanced back over their shoulders, in fear that they might be followed. Every stump that appeared along their path seemed an enemy and made them catch their breath.

"We have to get to the tannery!" Tom said in short catches between breaths. When they reached the tannery, they burst through the open door and fell, grateful and exhausted, into its sheltering shadows. After their pulses stopped racing, Tom whispered, "Huck, what do you reckon'll come of this?"

"If Dr. Robinson dies, I reckon hanging'll come of it."

Tom thought awhile, then said, "Who'll tell? Us?"

"What are you talkin' about? S'pose something happened and Injun Joe *didn't* hang. He'd kill us some time or other."

"That's what I was thinking."

"If anybody tells, let Muff Potter do it. He's usually drunk enough."

Tom went on thinking. "Muff Potter don't *know* it. How can he tell?"

"What do you mean, he don't know it?"

"He'd just got knocked out when Injun Joe stabbed Dr. Robinson."

"By hokey, that's so, Tom."

"Besides, maybe that whack done for *him*!"

"Ain't likely, Tom. He had liquor in him. When Pap's drunk, you could belt him over the head with a church and it wouldn't phase him. It must be the same with Muff Potter."

"Huck, you sure you can keep mum?"

"We *got* to keep mum. Injun Joe would kill us

for sure if we squeaked 'bout this and they didn't hang him. Look here, Tom, let's swear to each other, swear to keep mum."

"I'm agreed. It's the best thing. Hold hands and swear that we . . ."

"No, that won't do for this. That's good enough for little rubbishy things, but there oughta be writing 'bout a big thing like this. And blood."

Tom's whole being applauded this idea. He picked up a clean shingle, took a fragment of red chalk from his pocket, held the shingle so that it was lit by moonlight, and scrawled these words: "Huck Finn and Tom Sawyer swears they will keep mum about this, and they wish they may drop down dead in their tracks if they ever tell." Huck was filled with admiration for Tom's writing ability.

Tom unwound the thread from one of his needles, and each boy pricked the ball of his thumb and squeezed out a drop of blood. After many squeezes, Tom managed to sign his initials, using the ball of his little finger as a pen. Then he showed Huck how to make an H and an F, and the oath was complete. They buried the shingle close to the wall, with some incantations.

A figure crept through a break in the ruined building's other end, but Tom and Huck didn't notice.

"Tom, does this keep us from *ever* telling?" Huck whispered.

"Of course it does. Whatever happens, we got

to keep mum. Otherwise, we'd drop down dead. Sh! What's that?"

"Sounds like hogs grunting. No, it's somebody snoring."

"Where is it?"

"I think it's down at the other end."

The spirit of adventure rose once more within the boys' souls. "Do you dare to go if I lead?" Tom asked.

"S'pose it's Injun Joe!"

Tom quailed. But temptation soon returned, and the boys agreed to try, with the understanding that they would take to their heels if the snoring stopped. So they tiptoed down, one behind the other. When they were within five steps of the snorer, Tom stepped on a stick, and it broke with a snap. The man moaned and writhed a little. His face came into the moonlight. It was Potter. The boys' fears passed away now. They tiptoed out and stopped at a little distance to exchange a parting word.

When Tom crept in at his bedroom window, the night almost was over. He undressed with excessive caution and fell asleep congratulating himself that no one knew of his adventure. He was not aware that Sid had been awake for an hour.

Chapter 8

When Tom awoke, Sid was dressed and gone. The light of day had a late look. Tom was startled. Why hadn't he been called? Usually he was persecuted until he was up. Within five minutes he was dressed and downstairs. The family had finished breakfast but still sat around the table. No one expressed any rebuke. All eyes looked away. There was a silent solemnity that struck a chill to the culprit's heart. Tom sat down and tried to seem gay, but it was uphill work. There was no response, and he lapsed into silence.

After breakfast his aunt took him aside, wept, and asked him how he could break her old heart so. This was worse than a thousand whippings. He cried, pleaded for forgiveness, promised to reform, and received his dismissal. He left too miserable to even feel vengeful toward Sid, whose prompt retreat through the back gate was therefore unnecessary.

Tom moped to school. Along with Joe Harper, he was flogged for playing hooky the day before.

Tom took his flogging with the air of one whose heart was busy with heavier woes. Then he went to his seat, rested his elbows on his desk and his jaws in his hands, and stared at the wall with the stony stare of one who's suffering can get no worse. But it did get worse. He noticed something on his desk rolled in paper, unrolled it, and saw the brass knob that he had given to Becky.

About noon the ghastly news electrified the town. The tale flew from person to person, group to group, house to house, with little less than telegraphic speed. Dobbins made that afternoon a school holiday. The town would have disapproved if he hadn't.

A gory knife had been found close to the murdered man, and someone had recognized it as Muff Potter's. It was said that a citizen had come upon Potter washing himself in a stream about one o'clock in the morning and that Potter had immediately sneaked off—suspicious circumstances, especially the washing, which was not one of Potter's habits. It also was said that the town had been ransacked for this "murderer" (the public is quick when it comes to arriving at a verdict) but that he couldn't be found. Horsemen had departed in every direction, and the sheriff was "confident" that Potter would be captured before nightfall.

The whole town was drifting toward the graveyard. Tom's heartbreak vanished and he joined the procession, drawn by fascination. At the dreadful place, he squeezed through the crowd and beheld the dismal spectacle. It seemed an age since he had been there. Someone pinched his arm. He turned, and his eyes met Huck's. Both boys immediately looked away, wondering if anyone had noticed anything in their mutual glance. But everybody was talking, intent on the grisly spectacle.

"Poor young fellow. This ought to be a lesson to grave robbers. Muff Potter'll hang for this." This was the gist of the remarks. "It was a judgment," Reverend Sprague said. "The hand of the Lord is here."

Tom shivered as his eyes fell upon the emotionless face of Injun Joe.

The crowd began to sway, struggle, and shout. "It's him! He's coming. It's Muff Potter! He's stopped. He's turning. Don't let him get away!"

Someone in the tree branches over Tom's head said that Potter didn't look as if he was trying to get away, that he only looked confused.

"Infernal impudence!" someone else said in response to this comment. "I reckon Potter wanted to come and look at his work. He didn't expect any company."

The crowd fell apart, and the sheriff came through, leading Potter by the arm. Potter looked haggard and frightened. When he stood before the murdered man, he shook, put his face in his hands, and burst into tears. "I didn't do it," he sobbed. "Upon my word, I didn't do it."

"Who's accused you?" someone shouted.

This shot reached its mark. Potter lifted his face and looked around with a hopeless expression. He saw Joe, and exclaimed, "Joe, you promised you'd never . . ."

"Is that your knife?" the sheriff asked, thrusting it before Potter.

Potter would have fallen if they hadn't caught him and eased him to the ground. Waving his nerveless hand with a defeated gesture, he said, "Tell 'em, Joe. Tell 'em. It ain't no use."

Tom and Huck stood silent and staring as Joe calmly lied. The boys expected that, any moment, the clear sky would deliver God's lightning upon his head. When Joe had finished and still stood alive and whole, their wavering impulse to break their oath and save the poor prisoner's life vanished, because the murderer clearly had sold himself to Satan, and it would be fatal to meddle with the property of such a power. The boys inwardly resolved to watch Joe nights, when opportunity should offer, in the hope of glimpsing his dread Master.

"Why didn't you leave? Why'd you come here?" someone asked.

"I couldn't help it," Potter moaned. "I wanted to run away, but I couldn't seem to come anywhere but here."

Joe repeated his false statement under oath, just as calmly, a few minutes later. He helped raise the body of the murdered man and put it into a wagon for removal. The shuddering crowd whispered that the wound bled a little. The boys thought that this circumstance would turn suspicion in the right direction, but they were disappointed. More than one person remarked, "It was within three feet of Muff Potter when it bled."

Tom's conscience disturbed his sleep for a week after this. One morning at breakfast, Sid said, "Tom, you pitch around and talk in your sleep so much that you keep me awake half the time." Tom whitened and dropped his eyes.

"It's a bad sign," Aunt Polly said gravely. "What you got on your mind, Tom?"

"Nothing." But Tom's hand shook so much that he spilled his coffee.

"And you do talk such stuff!" Sid said. "Last night you said, 'It's blood; it's blood!' You said that over and over. And you said, 'Don't torment me so. I'll tell!' Tell *what*? What is it you'll tell?"

Tom felt dizzy. Without knowing it, Aunt Polly came to Tom's rescue by saying, "It's that dreadful murder. I dream about it 'most every night myself."

Mary said that she had been affected much the same way. Sid seemed satisfied. After that, Tom complained of toothache for a week so that he could silence himself by tying up his jaws every night. He didn't know that Sid lay watching him every night and frequently slipped the bandage off, leaned on his elbow listening for a good while, then slipped the bandage back on. Tom's distress gradually lessened, and the imaginary toothache grew annoying and was discarded. If Sid managed to make anything out of Tom's disjointed mutterings, he kept it to himself.

Tom's schoolmates held numerous "official" inquiries about dead cats, thus keeping alive Tom's troubled thoughts. Sid noticed that Tom never headed these inquiries, although it had been Tom's habit to take the lead in all new enterprises. Sid also noticed that Tom never acted as a witness; in fact, Tom avoided any participation in these inquiries. Finally, they went out of fashion.

Every day or two during this period, Tom went to the grated window of Potter's cell and passed small comforts to the "murderer." The jail was a small brick building at the town's edge. Partly because it seldom was occupied, it was unguarded. The offerings helped to ease Tom's conscience.

The townspeople had a strong desire to tar and feather Injun Joe for body snatching, but he was so feared that no one was willing to take the lead in the matter, so it was dropped.

Tom's mind drifted away from its secret troubles partly because it had another weighty matter to consider: Becky had stopped coming to school. She was ill. What if she died? Tom put his hoop, bat, and other playthings away; he took no pleasure in them anymore.

Concerned, Aunt Polly began to try all sorts of remedies on Tom. She subscribed to all the "health" magazines that offered worthless advice on how to breathe, what to eat and drink, how to get into bed, how to get out of bed, how to exercise, and how to think. She never noticed that the magazines of one month usually contradicted everything said in the magazines of the previous month. She was a firm believer in quack treatments. Using a new water treatment, she took Tom out to the woodshed every dawn and half drowned him in cold water. Then she scrubbed him, rolled him in a wet sheet, and kept him under blankets until he sweated his soul clean. Despite Aunt Polly's efforts, Tom grew more and more pale and dejected. So Aunt Polly added hot baths and showers. Tom remained as dismal as a hearse.

Tom actually took to reaching school ahead of time. Instead of playing with his comrades, he hung around the schoolyard gate. He would look down the road, hoping to see Becky. Whenever a frisking frock came into sight, his heart would leap until he saw it wasn't hers. Then, at last, it *was* hers. The next instant he was laughing, chasing boys, jumping over the fence, doing handsprings, and standing on his head—doing everything he could think of to impress Becky. But she never looked. So he moved his exploits to her immediate vicinity. He war-whooped; snatched a boy's cap and hurled it up to the schoolhouse roof; broke through a group of boys, tumbling them in every direction; and fell sprawling under Becky's nose, almost knocking Becky down. She turned, her nose in the air, and said, "Hmph! Some people think they're mighty smart. Always showing off."

Tom gathered himself up and sneaked off, crushed.

Chapter 9

When Tom next encountered his friend Joe Harper, he started blubbering about being unloved and ill-used. He would go off and never return, he said. He hoped that Joe would remember him. Joe had been looking for Tom to say much the same. His mother had whipped him for drinking some cream that he knew nothing about. It was clear that she was tired of him and wished him gone. He hoped that she would be happy and never regret having driven her poor boy out into the unfeeling world to suffer and die. The two boys swore to stand by each other and never part until death ended their sorrows. Then they discussed what to do. Joe proposed being hermits and living on crusts in some remote cave, but Tom convinced him that it would be better to be pirates.

They chose Jackson's Island as their base—a narrow, wooded, uninhabited island three miles below St. Petersburg, in the Mississippi River. Then they found Huck, who promptly agreed to join them. Before separating, the boys arranged to meet, at midnight, at a lonely spot on the river-bank two miles above the town. There was a small log raft there that they intended to "borrow." Each of them would bring hooks, lines, and (as suited outlaws) whatever provisions he could steal.

Around midnight Tom arrived with a boiled ham and a few trifles. He stopped in a dense undergrowth on a small bluff overlooking the meeting place. The mighty Mississippi lay like an ocean at rest. No sound disturbed the quiet. Tom gave a low, distinct whistle.

It was answered from under the bluff. "Who goes there?" a guarded voice asked.

"Tom Sawyer, Black Avenger of the Spanish Main. State your names."

"Huck Finn the Red-Handed and Joe Harper, Terror of the Seas." Tom had furnished these titles from his favorite literature.

"Give the countersign."

Together, Huck and Joe said, "Blood."

Tom tumbled his ham over the bluff and let himself down after it, tearing his clothes and skin. There was an easy, comfortable path along the shore under the bluff, but it lacked the danger that a pirate values.

The Terror of the Seas had brought a side of bacon and had just about worn himself out getting it there. Finn the Red-Handed had stolen a frying pan and some tobacco. He also had brought a few corn cobs with which to make pipes. But he was the only pirate who chewed or smoked tobacco. The Black Avenger said that they must start with a fire. They saw a fire smoldering on a large raft a hundred yards away. So, knowing that all of the raftsmen were down at the town, they helped themselves to a chunk. Then they shoved off, with Tom in command, Huck at the rear oar, and Joe at the front one.

Tom stood with folded arms and gave his orders in a low, stern voice. "Bring her to the wind."

"Aye aye, sir."

"Steady, steady."

"Steady it is, sir."

Such orders were given only for style. In reality, the boys monotonously drove the raft toward the river's middle.

Hardly a word was said during the next hour. The raft passed the distant town. A few glimmering lights showed where it lay, peacefully sleeping beyond the vast sweep of star-gemmed water. About two o'clock in the morning the raft grounded two hundred yards above the head of Jackson's Island, and the boys waded back and forth until they had landed their freight. Part of the little raft's belongings consisted of an old sail. They spread this over a nook in some bushes, as a tent to shelter their provisions. They themselves would sleep in the open air, as suited outlaws.

They built a fire alongside a large log about twenty steps inside the forest. Then they cooked some bacon in the frying pan and used up half of their cornbread. It was glorious to feast on an unexplored, uninhabited island. The boys agreed that they never would return to civilization. The fire lit their faces and threw its reddish glare on tree trunks and vines. When the last crisp slice of bacon was gone and the last cornbread devoured, the boys contentedly stretched on the grass.

"Ain't it great?" Joe said.

"Yep," Tom said. "What would the boys say if they could see us?"

"They'd just die to be here. Right, Huck?"

"I reckon so," Huck said. "I don't want nothing better 'n this. I don't ever get enough to eat, generally. And here they can't come and bully a feller."

"It's the life for me," Tom said. "You don't have to get up mornings, go to school, wash, and all that blame foolishness. A pirate don't have to do *anything*."

"What *does* pirates do?" the Red-Handed asked. Having carved out a cob, he loaded the "pipe" with tobacco, lit it with a hot coal, and blew a cloud of fragrant smoke. He was utterly content. The other pirates envied him this majestic vice and secretly resolved to acquire it soon.

"They just have a great time," Tom said. "They capture ships and burn them, and get the money and bury it in island places where there's ghosts and things to watch it. They kill everybody on the ships, make 'em walk a plank."

"They don't kill the women, though," Joe said. "They carry the women to their island."

"No, they don't kill the women," Tom agreed. "They're too noble. And the women's always beautiful."

"And don't pirates wear the best clothes!" Joe exclaimed. "All gold and silver and diamonds."

Huck scanned his own clothes. "I reckon I ain't dressed like a pirate," he said. "I ain't got no clothes but these."

Tom and Joe told him that fine clothes would come soon enough, after they began their adventures. They assured him that his rags would do for now, although it was customary for pirates to start with a proper wardrobe.

Gradually the talk died out and drowsiness overcame the boys, but only the Red-Handed quickly fell asleep. The Black Avenger and Terror of the Seas said their prayers silently and lying down because there was no one there to make them recite and kneel. Then, when they hovered on the verge of sleep, conscience intruded. They began to fear that they had done something wrong in running away. Next they thought of the stolen meat. They tried to argue their doubts away by reminding themselves that they had taken sweetmeats dozens of times, but there was no getting around the fact that taking sweetmeats was only filching whereas taking hams and such was *stealing*, and there was a command against that in the Bible. They inwardly vowed that their piracies would not again be stained with the crime of stealing. Having thus made their peace with conscience, these inconsistent pirates fell asleep.

When Tom awoke in the morning, he wondered where he was. He sat up, rubbed his eyes, and looked around. Then he remembered. It was a cool, gray dawn. The silent woods were wonderfully peaceful. Dewdrops beaded the leaves and grass. A white layer of ashes covered the fire, and a thin breath of blue smoke rose into the air. Joe and Huck still slept. Far away in the woods a bird called. Another answered. A woodpecker hammered. Gradually the morning's gray lightened to white, and sounds multiplied. A little green worm crawled over a dewy leaf, lifting two-thirds of her body into the air from time to time, "sniffing around," then continuing on. When the worm approached Tom, he sat still as a stone. She dropped onto his leg and journeyed over him. Tom rejoiced because that meant that he would have a new suit of clothes— without a doubt, a pirate outfit.

A procession of ants went about their labors. One struggled with a dead spider five times her size, lugging the body straight up a tree. A lady bug climbed a grass blade, then took wing. A tumble-bug heaved his ball. Tom touched the creature, who shut his legs against his body, pretending to be dead. A catbird landed in a tree over Tom's head and trilled out a rapturous song. Then a shrill jay swept down—a flash of blue flame—paused on a twig almost within Tom's reach, cocked his head to one side, and eyed the strangers with curiosity. A gray squirrel came scurrying along, sitting up at intervals to inspect and chatter at the boys. A few butterflies came fluttering. Nature was wide awake now. Far and near, long sunbeams pierced the dense foliage.

Tom roused the other pirates. In about a minute they all were stripped. They chased and tumbled over each other in the white sandbar's shallow water. They felt no longing for the little town sleeping in the distance. A slight rise in the river had carried off their raft, but this pleased them because its departure seemed to burn the bridge between them and civilization.

They returned to camp refreshed, merry, and hungry. They soon had the campfire blazing. Huck found a spring of clear, cold water close by, and the boys made cups out of broad leaves. Water, sweetened with such wildwood charm, was a good substitute for coffee. When Joe began to slice bacon for breakfast, Tom and Huck asked him to wait a minute. They stepped to a promising nook in the riverbank and threw in their lines. Joe hadn't had time to get impatient when they returned with some handsome bass, a couple of sun perch, and a small catfish—provisions enough for a family. They fried the fish with the bacon. No fish ever had seemed so delicious.

After breakfast they lay around in the shade. Huck had a smoke. Then the boys went off to explore the woods. They tramped gaily along, over decaying logs, through tangled underbrush, past drooping grapevines and snug nooks carpeted with grass and decorated with flowers. The island, they found, was about three miles long and a quarter of a mile wide. A channel scarcely two hundred yards wide separated it from the shore. The boys took a swim about every hour, so it was mid-afternoon when they returned to camp.

They dined on cold ham, then threw themselves down in the shade to talk. But the talk soon dragged and then died. The place's stillness and isolation started to weigh on the boys. Each started to feel homesick. Even Finn the Red-Handed longed for his doorsteps and empty barrels. But they all were ashamed of their weakness, so none revealed his thoughts.

For some time the boys had been half conscious of a peculiar sound in the distance. Now this odd sound became more pronounced. The boys started, glanced at one another, and listened. After a long silence a deep boom floated down from a distance.

"What is it?" Joe asked.

"I wonder," Tom said.

"Ain't thunder," Huck said, "'cause thunder . . ."

"Hush!" Tom said.

They waited. The muffled boom came again.

"Let's go and see."

They sprang to their feet and hurried to the shore toward the town. Parting the bushes on the bank, they peered out over the water. The steam ferryboat was about a mile below the town, drifting with the current. Its deck was crowded with people. Many skiffs rowed about or floated with the stream near the ferry, but the boys couldn't determine what the people in them were doing. A large jet of white smoke burst from the ferry's side. As it expanded and rose in a lazy cloud, the dull throb sounded again.

"I know now!" Tom exclaimed. "Somebody's drownded."

"That's it," Huck said. "They done that last summer when Bill Turner drownded. They shoot a cannon over the water, and that makes the body come up to the top."

"By jings, I wish I was there," Joe said.

"Me too," Huck said. "I'd give heaps to know who it is."

The boys continued to listen and watch. Then a thought flashed through Tom's mind and he exclaimed, "I know who drownded! It's us!"

The boys instantly felt like heroes. This was a gorgeous triumph. They were missed. They were mourned. Hearts were breaking on their account.

People were feeling remorse over their unkindness to these poor lost lads. Best of all, the departed were the talk of the town.

As twilight approached, the ferry returned to its usual business and the skiffs disappeared. The pirates returned to camp. They were jubilant over their new grandeur and the trouble they were causing. They caught fish, cooked supper, and ate it, then fell to guessing what the town was thinking and saying about them. But when night closed in, they gradually ceased to talk. They sat gazing into the fire and started thinking about people back home who were not enjoying the situation as much as they were. Their misgivings grew. A sigh or two escaped. Joe timidly asked how the others might feel about returning to civilization—not right now but . . .

Tom withered him with derision. Huck joined in. Joe quickly "explained" and was glad to get out of the scrape with as little taint of cowardly homesickness clinging to his garments as he could. For the moment, mutiny was laid to rest.

As the night deepened, Huck began to nod and then to snore. Joe followed. Tom lay on his elbow, motionless, for some time, watching the two. At last he cautiously got up onto his knees and searched, by the light of the flickering campfire, through the grass. He picked up and inspected several pieces of thin white bark and chose two. Then he knelt by the fire and wrote on each with his red chalk. He rolled one up and put it into his jacket pocket. The other he put into Joe's hat, which he moved a little distance from its owner. He also put into the hat some treasures of inestimable value—among them, a lump of white chalk, a rubber ball, three fishhooks, and a clear marble. He tiptoed among the trees until he thought he was out of hearing. Then he ran toward the sandbar.

A few minutes later Tom was in the sandbar's shallow water, wading toward the Illinois shore. Before the depth reached his middle, he was halfway over. The current would permit no more wading, so he swam the remaining hundred yards. He drifted along until he found a low place and pulled himself out. He put his hand on his jacket pocket, found that his piece of bark was safe, and struck through the woods with streaming garments, following the shore.

Shortly before ten o'clock he reached an open place opposite the town and saw the ferry lying in the shadow of the trees and high bank. Everything was quiet under the stars. He crept down the bank, slipped into the water, swam several strokes, and climbed into the skiff at the boat's stern. He lay down under the bench-like seat and waited.

The cracked bell rang, and a voice gave the order to cast off. A minute later the skiff's head was standing high up, against the boat's swell, and the voyage had begun. Tom was happy in his success;

it was the boat's last trip for the night. After a long fifteen minutes or so, the wheels stopped and Tom slipped overboard and swam ashore in the dusk, landing fifty yards downstream.

He flew down unfrequented alleys and soon found himself at his aunt's back fence. He climbed over and looked in through the window of the sitting room, where a light was burning. There sat Aunt Polly, Sid, Mary, and Sereny Harper, talking. They were by the bed, which stood between them and the door. Tom went to the door, softly lifted the latch, and gently pressed. The door yielded a crack. He continued pushing cautiously, quaking every time it creaked. When the crack was big enough, he crawled through.

"What's making the candle blow?" Aunt Polly asked. Tom hurried. "Why, that door's open. Go shut it, Sid."

Tom disappeared under the bed, then crept to where he almost could touch his aunt's foot.

"As I was saying," Aunt Polly said, "he warn't bad, just mischievous. He warn't any more responsible than a colt, but he never meant any harm. He was the best-hearted boy that ever . . ." She started to cry.

"My Joe was the same—up to every kind of mischief but as kind as could be," Sereny Harper said. "To think that I went and whipped him for taking that cream, not recollecting that I throwed it out myself because it was sour. And I'm never to see him again in this world. Never! Poor abused boy!" She sobbed.

"I hope Tom's better off where he is," Sid said, "but if he'd been better in some ways . . ."

"Sid!" Tom felt the glare of Aunt Polly's eyes, though he couldn't see them. "Not a word against my Tom now that he's gone. Oh, Sereny, I don't know how to give him up! He was such a comfort to me, even though he 'most tormented my old heart out of me."

"Only last Saturday my Joe busted a firecracker right under my nose, and I knocked him sprawling. Little did I know how soon . . . Oh, if I had it to do over again, I'd hug him and bless him for it."

"I know just how you feel." Aunt Polly broke down.

Tom was sniffling himself now, more out of pity for himself than anyone else. He could hear Mary crying and putting in a kindly word for him from time to time. He began to have a nobler opinion of himself than ever before. He was sufficiently touched by his aunt's grief to long to rush out from under the bed and overwhelm his aunt with joy. The theatrical gorgeousness of such an entrance also appealed strongly to him, but he resisted.

He went on listening and gathered, from snippets, that the boys were believed to have drowned while swimming. The small raft had been found lodged against the Missouri shore about five miles below the town. It was believed that the search for the bodies had failed because the boys had drowned mid-channel; otherwise, being good swimmers, they would have made it to the shore. This was Wednesday night. If the boys still were missing on Sunday, all hope would be gone and the funerals would be preached that morning. Tom shuddered.

Sereny Harper sobbed, "Good night," and turned to go. Then, with a mutual impulse, the two bereaved women flung themselves into each other's arms. After a good, consoling cry, they parted. Sid sniffled a bit, and Mary went off crying with all her heart. Aunt Polly knelt and prayed for Tom with such love in her words and her trembling voice, that he dripped with tears again. He had to keep still long after she went to bed, because she cried out from time to time and tossed and turned. At last she only moaned a little in her sleep.

Tom stole out from under the bed and, shading the candlelight with his hand, stood looking at her. His heart was full of pity. He took out his piece of bark and placed it by the candle. Then his face lit with a happy thought, and he returned the bark to his pocket. He bent over, kissed his aunt's faded lips, and left, latching the door behind him.

Tom threaded his way back to the ferry and walked boldly on board. He knew that no one else was there except the watchman, who always slept like a statue. Tom untied the skiff, slipped into it, and soon was rowing upstream. When he stepped ashore, he entered the woods and took a long rest before starting for the camp. It was broad daylight before he found himself at the island sandbar. He rested again until the sun gilded the great river. Then he plunged into the stream. A little later he paused, dripping, at the camp's threshold. He heard Joe say, "Tom's true blue, Huck. He'll be back. He knows that an honorable pirate doesn't desert."

"Well, the things is ours anyway, ain't they?"

"Not yet, Huck. The writing says they're ours if he ain't back for breakfast."

"Which he is!" Tom exclaimed with fine dramatic effect, stepping grandly into camp.

A sumptuous breakfast of bacon and fish soon was provided. As the boys set to work on it, Tom recounted (and adorned) his adventures. They were a vain, boastful trio by the time the tale was done.

Tom hid himself in a shady nook to sleep until noon, and the other pirates got ready to fish and explore.

After lunch the boys looked for turtle eggs on the sandbar. They poked sticks into the sand. When they found a soft place, they dropped to their knees and dug with their hands. Sometimes they took fifty or sixty small, round white eggs from one hole. They feasted on fried eggs that night and on Friday morning.

After Friday's breakfast they alternately chased one another, splashed and ducked one another, and sprawled on the dry, hot sand. Gradually they wandered apart and fell to gazing across the river to the town. Tom wrote "Becky" in the sand with his big toe, then was angry with himself for his weakness and scratched it out.

By the time the boys got back together, Joe was so homesick that he nearly was crying. Huck and Tom were downhearted, too. With a false show of cheerfulness, Tom said, "I bet there's been pirates on this island before. Let's explore it again. They've hid treasure here somewhere. How'd you like to find a chest full of gold and silver?"

No one replied. Joe sat poking the sand with a stick. Finally he said, "Let's give it up. I want to go home."

"You'll feel better soon, Joe. Just think of the fishing that's here," Tom said.

"I don't like fishing. I want to go home."

"But, Joe, there ain't such a good swimming place anywhere."

"I don't seem to like swimming when there ain't anybody to forbid it. I'm goin' home."

"Baby! You want to see your mother."

"Yes, I do want to see my mother, and you would too if you had one." Joe sniffled a bit.

"Well, we'll let the cry-baby go home to his mother, won't we, Huck? *You* like it here, don't you, Huck? We'll stay, won't we?"

Huck answered, "Yes," without any heart in it.

"I'll never speak to you again as long as I live," Joe said, getting up.

"Who cares?" Tom responded.

Joe gathered his things and, without a parting word, waded off toward the Illinois shore.

"I want to go, too, Tom," Huck said. "It was getting lonesome before, and now it'll be worse. Let's go, too."

"I'm stayin'. You can go if you want to."

Huck started after Joe. Tom hoped that the boys would stop, but they waded on. Suddenly Tom darted after his comrades, yelling, "Wait! I want to tell you something."

Joe and Huck stopped and turned around. When Tom reached them, he revealed a plan related to what he had overheard back at his house. Joe and Huck whooped with appreciation. They said the situation was "splendid" and that if Tom had revealed his plan before, they wouldn't have started to leave. All three boys came gaily back and resumed their sport, chattering all the time about Tom's stupendous plan and admiring its genius.

After a dinner of eggs and fish, Tom said that he wanted to learn to smoke. Joe said that he would like to try, too. So Huck made pipes and filled them. Tom and Joe stretched themselves out on their elbows and began to puff. The smoke had an unpleasant taste, and they gagged a little.

"I could smoke this pipe all day," Joe said. "I

don't feel sick."

"Neither do I," Tom said. "I could smoke it all day, too, but I bet Davey Thatcher couldn't."

"Davey Thatcher! Why, he'd keel over after just two puffs."

"So would Johnny Miller."

"Just one little puff would finish *him*," Joe agreed.

"I wish the boys could see us now," Tom said.

"Me, too."

So the talk ran on. But it soon flagged. The silences widened, and the spitting increased until it reached a rapid pace. The pores inside the boys' cheeks became spouting fountains that overflowed down their throats. Both boys looked pale and miserable now. Their pipes soon dropped from their nerveless fingers.

"I've lost my knife," Joe said weakly. "I better go find it."

With quivering lips and halting utterance, Tom said, "I'll help you. You go over that way, and I'll look around by the spring. You needn't come, Huck; we can find it."

Huck waited an hour before going to find his comrades. They were wide apart in the woods, both very pale and fast asleep. They had retched away their problem.

Tom and Joe were not talkative at supper. They had a humble look. When Huck prepared his pipe after the meal and was going to prepare theirs, they said no, they were not feeling very well; something they had eaten at supper had disagreed with them.

About midnight Joe awoke and roused the others. A quivering glow vaguely revealed the foliage for a moment and then vanished. Another followed, somewhat stronger. Then another. Then a flash turned night into day and showed every grass blade, separate and distinct. It also shone on three startled faces. A deep roll of thunder rumbled and faded. Chilly air swept by, rustling the leaves and blowing the fire's flaky ashes. Another fierce glare lit the forest. A crash followed that seemed to rend the treetops right over the boys' heads. The boys clung together in terror in the thick gloom. A few large raindrops plopped onto the leaves. "Quick! Go for the tent!" Tom exclaimed. They sprang away, stumbling over roots and among vines in the dark. No two plunged in the same direction. A furious blast roared through the trees. One blinding flash followed another, and peal after peal of deafening thunder. A drenching rain poured down. The rising hurricane drove it in sheets along the ground. The boys cried out to each other, but the roaring wind and booming thunder drowned out their voices.

One by one they straggled in and took shelter under the tent—cold, scared, and streaming with water. The storm and the tent's flapping made so much noise that they couldn't talk. The tempest rose higher and higher. The tent tore loose and flew away. The boys seized one another's hands and fled, with tumblings and bruisings, to the shelter of a great oak that stood on the riverbank. Ceaseless lightning flamed in the skies. Everything below stood out sharp and shadowless: the bending trees, the billowing river, the high bluffs in the distance. Clouds drifted rapidly, and rain fell in a slanting veil. Every little while a giant tree snapped and crashed to the ground. Unflagging thunder pealed in appalling, ear-splitting bursts.

At last the fearsome threat retreated. Peace returned, and the boys returned to camp. They found that a great sycamore had crashed where their tent had been, so they felt grateful that they had fled. Everything in their camp—including the fire—was drenched. They were soaked and chilled. But then they discovered that, under a log, remnants of the fire had escaped wetting, so they managed to restore the fire. They dried their boiled ham and had a feast. Then they sat by the fire and glorified and embellished their midnight adventure until morning because there was no dry spot on which to sleep.

As the sun stole in on the boys, they became drowsy. They went to the sandbar and lay down to sleep. By and by, the heat was too scorching, so they drearily set about getting breakfast. After the meal they felt stiff and homesick. Good cheer returned when Tom proposed that they stop being

pirates for a while and become Indians instead—
all of them chiefs, of course. They stripped, striped
themselves from head to heel with black mud, and
went tearing through the woods to attack an
English settlement. Next they separated into three
hostile tribes and ambushed one another. With
dreadful war whoops, they killed and scalped one
another by the thousands. It was a gory day, con-
sequently an extremely satisfying one.

They assembled in camp toward suppertime,
hungry and happy. We will leave them, for now, to
chatter and brag.

Chapter 10

There was no joy in St. Petersburg that same peaceful Saturday afternoon. The Harpers and Aunt Polly's family were in mourning. The town's residents talked little and sighed often. The children had no heart for playing. In the afternoon Becky Thatcher moped around the deserted schoolyard. She thought, "If only I'd kept the brass knob! Now I have nothing to remember him by. I'll never see him again." Tears rolled down her cheeks. A group of Tom and Joe's playmates stood looking over Aunt Polly's fence and recalling, in reverent tones, things that Tom and Joe had said and done—things that, they now realized, had foretold the boys' deaths. There was a dispute regarding who had last seen Tom and Joe alive. Many claimed that dismal distinction. When it was finally decided who had seen them last, and exchanged the last words with them, the lucky parties acquired a sort of sacred importance and were gaped at and envied by the rest.

The next morning, when Sunday school concluded, the church's bell began to toll. The townspeople began to gather, pausing a moment in the lobby to whisper about the sad event. At the pews, there was no whispering; only the rustling of funeral dresses disturbed the silence there. No one could remember a time when the little church had been so full. Following an expectant pause, Aunt Polly entered, then Sid and Mary, then the Harper family, all in black. Reverend Sprague and the congregation respectfully rose and remained standing until the mourners were seated in the front pew. There was another communing silence, broken at intervals by muffled sobs. Then Reverend Sprague spread his hands and prayed. A moving hymn was sung, followed by the text "I am the Resurrection and the Life."

As the service proceeded, Reverend Sprague drew such pictures of the lost lads' graces, winning ways, and rare promise that everyone present felt a pang at never having noticed those virtues in the boys. Reverend Sprague related many touching incidents that illustrated the sweet, generous natures of the departed. The people easily could see—now—how noble and beautiful those incidents had been, although at the time that they had occurred they had seemed the worst rascalness. At last the whole company produced a chorus of sobs. Even Reverend Sprague wept.

When the church door creaked, Reverend

Sprague raised his streaming eyes above his hand-kerchief and stood transfixed. One pair of eyes after another followed his. Then, almost with one impulse, the congregation rose and stared. The three dead boys came marching up the aisle—Tom in the lead, Joe next, and Huck sneaking shyly in the rear. They had been hiding in the vacant gallery listening to their own funeral.

Aunt Polly, Mary, and the Harpers threw themselves on their restored ones, smothered them with kisses, and poured out thanksgivings. Huck was tremendously uncomfortable. He started to slink away, but Tom grabbed him and said, "Aunt Polly, it ain't fair. Somebody's got to be glad to see Huck."

"I'm glad to see him, poor motherless thing!" The loving attentions that Aunt Polly lavished on Huck made him even more uncomfortable than he had been before.

Reverend Sprague shouted, "Praise God, from whom all blessings flow! Sing!"

And they did. The triumphant burst shook the rafters. Tom looked around at all the envious boys and girls and gloried in this, the proudest moment of his life.

That day Tom got more kisses and cuffs (depending on Aunt Polly's changing moods) than he ever had in an entire year.

It had been Tom's idea that the boys return home just in time to attend their own funeral.

Saturday at dusk they had paddled to the Missouri shore on a log, landing about five miles below the town. They had slept in the woods at the town's edge until it nearly was daylight. Then they had crept through back lanes and alleys and finished their sleep in the church's gallery.

Monday morning at breakfast, Aunt Polly and Mary were very loving to Tom and very attentive to his wants. There was an unusual amount of talk. In the course of it, Aunt Polly said, "Well, I don't say it wasn't a fine joke, Tom, to keep everybody suffering 'most a week while you boys had a good time. But it's a pity you could be hardhearted enough to let *me* suffer so. If you could come over on a log to go to your funeral, you could have come over and give me a hint that you warn't dead but only run off."

"Yes, you could have done that, Tom," Mary said.

"You'll look back some day, when it's too late, and wish you'd cared a little more for me," Aunt Polly said.

"Now, Auntie, you know that I care for you," Tom said.

"I'd know it better if you acted like you did."

"I wish now that I'd let you know I was alive," Tom said with a repentant tone. "But I dreamt about you. That's something, ain't it?"

"It ain't much. A cat does that much. But it's better than nothing. What did you dream?"

"Wednesday night I dreamt that you was sitting over there by the bed, and Sid was sitting by the firewood box, and Mary was next to him."

"Well, so we did. But we always do."

"And I dreamt that Mrs. Harper was here."

"Why, she *was*! Did you dream any more?"

"I think the wind blowed the candle."

"Mercy on us, it did! Go on, Tom."

"It seems to me that you told Sid to shut the door."

"I never heard the beat of that in all my days! Don't tell *me* there ain't anything in dreams. Sereny Harper will know of this before I'm an hour older. I'd like to see her call *this* superstition. Go on, Tom."

"You said I wasn't bad, only mischievous and no more responsible than . . . than . . . I think it was a colt."

"So it was!"

"Then you cried."

"So I did."

"Mrs. Harper cried, too. She said that Joe was the same way and that she wished she hadn't whipped him for taking cream when she'd throwed it out her own self."

"Tom, the spirit was upon you!"

To Aunt Polly's growing amazement, Tom continued to describe everything as it had happened. "I'm thankful to God I've got you back," Aunt Polly said.

As soon as Mary, Sid, and Tom left for school, Aunt Polly called on Sereny Harper, to demolish her realism with Tom's marvelous dream.

Sid had this thought, which he didn't express: "Pretty unbelievable—as long a dream as that without any mistakes in it!"

What a hero Tom was! He moved with a dignified swagger. The public eye was on him. Smaller boys flocked at his heels, proud to be seen with him. Boys of his own age were consumed with envy. They would have given anything to have his suntanned skin and glittering notoriety. At school, children made such a fuss over Tom and Joe, and looked at them so admiringly, that the two soon were insufferably stuck-up.

Tom decided that he no longer needed Becky Thatcher. Glory sufficed. When Becky arrived, Tom pretended not to see her. He joined a group of boys and girls and began to talk. Becky tripped gaily back and forth with flushed face and dancing eyes, pretending to be busy chasing schoolmates and screaming with laughter when she made a capture. Tom noticed that she made her captures in his vicinity while looking in his direction. This gratified his vanity.

Finally Becky gave up and moved away, glancing wistfully toward Tom. Then she noticed that Tom was talking more to Amy Lawrence than to anyone else. She felt a sharp pang. She moved to the group and announced, almost at Tom's elbow, that her mother was planning a picnic for her: "She'll let anybody come that I want." The entire group begged for invitations—except for Tom and Amy. Tom turned away coolly, still talking to Amy. Becky's lips trembled. Becky got away as soon as she could, hid herself, and cried. Then she sat with wounded pride until the bell rang, at which point she roused herself, gave her braids a shake, and determined to get revenge.

At recess Tom continued flirting with Amy. He drifted in search of Becky, so that he could sting her with his performance. When he spotted her, his spirits took a dive. She was sitting on a bench with Alfred Temple. They were looking at a picture book with such absorption that they didn't seem conscious of anything else in the world. Their heads were so close together that they almost touched.

Jealousy ran red-hot through Tom's veins. Amy chatted happily as she and Tom walked along, but Tom's tongue had lost its function. Tom didn't hear what Amy was saying. Whenever she paused expectantly, he stammered an assent, whether or not it made sense. He kept returning to the bench where Becky and Alfred sat, to sear his eyeballs with the hateful spectacle. Becky noticed and was glad to see him suffer.

Amy's happy prattle became intolerable. Tom said that he had some things to attend to and hurried away. "Any other boy!" Tom thought, grating his teeth. "Any boy in the whole town but that St.

Louis smarty that dresses so fine and thinks he's an aristocrat. I licked him the day he came to this town, and I'll lick him again." He went through the motions of thrashing a boy—pounding the air, kicking, and gouging.

At noon Tom fled. Becky resumed her picture inspections with Alfred, but when no Tom came to suffer, she lost interest and grew miserable. Poor Alfred kept exclaiming, "Oh, here's a jolly one. Look at this." Becky lost patience, said "Oh, don't bother me," and walked away.

Angry and humiliated, Alfred went inside the deserted schoolhouse and contemplated the situation. He quickly guessed the truth: Becky had used him to make Tom Sawyer jealous. He wished there was some way to get Tom into trouble. He noticed Tom's spelling book. He opened to the lesson for that afternoon and poured ink onto the page. Glancing in through a window, Becky saw the action. She started home, intending to tell Tom, who would be grateful. However, before she was halfway, she changed her mind. The memory of Tom's treatment of her came scorching back. She resolved to let Tom get whipped for the damaged spelling book and also to hate him forever.

Tom arrived home in a dreary mood. He had brought his sorrows to an unpromising market. The first thing his aunt said was, "Tom, I've a notion to skin you alive."

"What have I done, Auntie?"

"I went over to Sereny Harper and lorded that dream over her. Lo and behold, she'd found out from Joe that you was over here and heard all our talk that night. It makes me feel so bad that you could let me go to Sereny Harper and make such a fool of myself."

Tom felt ashamed. "Auntie, I wish I hadn't done it. I didn't think."

"Child, you never think of anything but your own self. You could think to come all the way from Jackson's Island to laugh at our sorrow. You could think to fool me with a lie about a dream. But you couldn't think to pity us and end our sorrow."

"Auntie, I know now that it was mean. I didn't mean to be mean. Besides, I didn't come here to laugh at you that night."

"Why'd you come, then?"

"It was to tell you not to worry because we hadn't drownded."

"I'd give the world to believe that, but why didn't you tell me, then?"

"I got all full of the idea of our coming and hiding in the church for the funeral, so I put the bark back in my pocket and kept mum."

"What bark?"

"The bark I had wrote on to tell you we'd gone pirating. I wish now that you'd waked up when I kissed you."

Tenderness came into Aunt Polly's eyes. "*Did* you kiss me, Tom?"

"Yes."

"Why?"

"Because I loved you so much, and you laid there moaning, and I was sorry."

The words sounded like truth. With a tremor in her voice, Aunt Polly said, "Kiss me again, Tom. And be off to school now."

The moment he was gone, she ran to a closet and got out the ruined jacket in which Tom had gone pirating. She reached into the pocket. A moment later she was reading Tom's piece of bark through flowing tears and thinking, "I could forgive that boy now if he'd committed a million sins."

Aunt Polly's affection had restored Tom's happiness. On his way to school Tom encountered Becky. His mood always determined his manner, so he unhesitatingly ran up to her and said, "I acted mighty mean today, Becky. I'm sorry. I won't ever do that again. Let's make up, alright?"

Becky stopped and looked him scornfully in the face. "I'll thank you to keep to yourself, Thomas Sawyer. I'll never speak to you again." She passed on.

Tom was stunned. He moped into the school-yard wishing that Becky were a boy, so that he could trounce her. When he encountered her again, he delivered a stinging remark. She hurled one in return. In her hot resentment, Becky hardly could wait for school to start, so that she could see Tom get flogged for the damaged spelling book.

Silas Dobbins had reached middle age without realizing his ambition of becoming a doctor. Poverty had decreed that he rise no higher than a schoolmaster. Every day he took a mysterious book out of his desk and absorbed himself in it when no student was reciting. He kept that book under lock and key. There was not a pupil in the school who wasn't dying to glimpse it. Every boy and girl had a different theory about the nature of that book. Now, as Becky passed Dobbins' desk, she noticed that the key was in the lock. She glanced around and, finding herself alone, took out the book. The title, Professor Somebody's Anatomy, conveyed no information to her, so she began to turn the pages. She came upon a human figure, stark naked. At that moment Tom stepped in and caught a glimpse of the picture. Becky closed the book with such haste that she tore the picture. She thrust the book into the desk, turned the key, and said angrily, "Tom Sawyer, you're just as mean as can be, to sneak up on a person and look at what they're looking at."

"How could *I* know you was looking at any-thing?"

"You're going to tell on me, and I'll be whipped!" She ran from the schoolhouse.

Tom stood still, rather flustered by this out-burst. He thought, "Girls are so thin-skinned.

What's a whipping? Anyway, I ain't gonna tell old Dobbins on her. He'll ask who tore his book, and nobody'll answer. Then he'll do what he always does—ask one pupil after another. When he comes to the right person, he'll know it. Girls' faces always tell on them."

In a few moments Dobbins arrived and school started. Every time that Tom glanced at Becky, her face troubled him. He couldn't help pitying her. However, when Dobbins discovered the damage to Tom's spelling book, Tom focused on his own problem. Becky roused from her distress and showed considerable interest in the proceedings. Tom denied having spilled the ink, but Dobbins thought he was lying. Becky had thought that she would rejoice in Tom's predicament, but she didn't. She had an impulse to get up and tell on Alfred Temple, but she forced herself to keep silent, thinking that Tom planned to tell that she had torn Dobbins' book.

Tom took his whipping and returned to his seat not at all brokenhearted. He thought he might have spilled the ink unknowingly. He had denied spilling it because denial was customary, and he'd stuck to the denial out of principle.

An hour drifted by. Dobbins sat nodding in his throne. The air was drowsy with the hum of study. Dobbins straightened himself up, yawned, unlocked his desk, and took out his book. He settled himself in his chair to read. Tom shot a glance at Becky. She looked like a helpless rabbit with a gun leveled at her head. Instantly Tom forgot his quarrel with her. Dobbins opened the book. The next moment he faced the school. Every eye sank under his gaze, which smote even the innocent with fear. Dobbins gathered his wrath, then demanded, "Who tore this book?"

Silence. Dobbins searched one face after another for signs of guilt. "Benjamin Rogers, did you tear this book?"

A denial.

"Joseph Harper, did *you*?"

Another denial.

Tom's uneasiness grew under the slow torture of these proceedings. Dobbins scanned the ranks of boys, considered awhile, then turned to the girls. "Amy Lawrence?"

A shake of the head.

"Gracie Miller?"

Another head shake.

"Susan Harper?"

Another negative.

The next girl was Becky. "Rebecca Thatcher, did you tear . . . No, look me in the face."

Becky was white with fear.

"Did you tear this book?"

Tom sprang to his feet. "I done it!"

The school stared in amazement at this incredible folly. When Tom stepped forward to receive his punishment, the gratitude and adoration that shone in Becky's eyes were payment enough for a hundred floggings. Inspired by the splendor of his action, Tom made no outcry throughout the most merciless flogging that Dobbins ever had administered. Tom also received with indifference Dobbins' command to remain two hours after school. (Tom knew who would wait outside for him until his captivity was over.)

Tom went to bed that night planning revenge on Alfred Temple. With shame and repentance, Becky had told him everything. But Tom's longing for revenge soon gave way to pleasanter thoughts. Tom fell asleep with Becky's last words sounding dreamily in his ear: "Tom, how *could* you be so noble?"

Chapter 11

As vacation approached, Silas Dobbins became more severe and exacting than ever. He wanted the school to make a good showing on examination day. His cane and paddle seldom rested now. Only the oldest pupils escaped vigorous lashing. Under his wig Dobbins was completely bald, but there was no weakness in his muscles. Subjected to continual fear and suffering, the smaller boys plotted revenge. They enlisted the help of a sign painter's son. Dobbins boarded with this boy's family and had given the boy much reason to hate him. Dobbins always prepared himself for great occasions by getting drunk. The sign painter's son said that he would "manage the thing" when Dobbins reached the necessary drunken condition on exam day and napped in his chair.

When exam evening arrived, the schoolhouse was brilliantly lit and adorned with wreaths and garlands of leaves and flowers. Dobbins sat enthroned in his great chair on a raised platform, with his blackboard behind him. He looked tolerably mellow. The town's dignitaries and the pupils' parents occupied three rows of benches on each side of Dobbins and six rows in front of him. To his left, behind the rows of citizens, pupils who would take part in the evening's exercises sat on a spacious temporary platform: small boys, washed and dressed to an intolerable state of discomfort; gawky big boys; and girls and young ladies adorned with trinkets, pink and blue ribbons, and flowers in their hair. The rest of the house was filled with non-participating students.

The exercises began. A very small boy stood and bashfully recited, "You'd scarce expect one of my age to speak in public on the stage . . .," accompanying himself with painfully precise and spasmodic gestures. He got through safely and received a fine round of applause as he gave a manufactured bow and retired. A shamefaced little girl lisped, "Mary had a little lamb," performed a compassion-inspiring curtsy, got her share of applause, and sat down flushed and happy. Tom Sawyer stepped forward with conceited confidence and soared into the famous "Give me liberty or give me death" speech. He gestured with fine fury until, in the middle of the speech, he broke down. Stage fright suddenly had seized him. His legs shook, and he felt that he would choke. The audience was sympathetic but silent. Dobbins frowned. Tom struggled awhile and then retired, utterly defeated.

There was a weak attempt at applause, which died early.

"The Boy Stood on the Burning Deck" and other declamatory gems followed. Then there were reading exercises and a spelling contest. The small Latin class recited with honor.

For the evening's highlight, young ladies read their own compositions. In turn, each one stepped forward to the platform's edge, cleared her throat, held up her manuscript, and read, with labored attention to manner of expression. The themes were friendship, goodness, religion throughout history, and the like. The compositions featured showy "fine language" and annoying repetition of particularly prized words and phrases. (The number of compositions making generous use of the word "beauteous" was up to the usual average.) Every composition ended with a sermon. No matter what the subject, some moral was squeezed out of it. The more frivolous and self-centered the author, the longer and more self-righteous her sermon. From time to time during the readings, the audience whispered, "How sweet!" "How eloquent!" or "How true!" One manuscript concluded with a sermon so damning of all non-Presbyterians that it won first prize.

Dobbins, drunk almost to the verge of geniality, put his chair aside, turned his back to the audience, and began to draw a map of America on the blackboard, to test the geography class. His unsteady hand made a sad business of it, and a smothered titter rippled through the house. He became entirely absorbed in drawing, erasing, and redrawing. The titters increased.

Over Dobbins' head was a garret with an opening. Through this opening, suspended by a rope around his haunches, a cat slowly descended. Down, down he came. Now he was within six inches of Dobbins' head. A little lower. The cat grabbed Dobbins' wig with his claws and was pulled back up into the garret with the trophy still in his possession. Light blazed from Dobbins' bald head. The sign painter's son had gilded it!

Laughter broke up the meeting. The boys were avenged, and vacation began.

Chapter 12

Vacation started out much duller than Tom had expected. He attempted a diary, but nothing happened three days in a row, so he abandoned it. Even the Fourth of July was a failure; it rained hard, so there was no parade. Some boys and girls had parties, but they were so few and so delightful that they only made the achy voids between them more achy. Becky had returned to her parents' Constantinople home for vacation, so the world was without charm.

Then the murder trial began. The entire town talked about it. Every reference to the murder made Tom shudder. His fears and troubled conscience almost persuaded him that people discussed the trial in his presence in order to see his reaction, as a kind of test. He took Huck to a lonely place to have a talk with him and assure himself that Huck had kept their secret.

"Huck, have you told anybody about . . . *it*?"

"What's *it*?"

"You know what."

"Oh! Course I haven't. What makes you ask?"

"Well, I was afeard."

"We wouldn't be alive two days if that got out," Huck said.

"I reckon we're safe as long as we keep mum. Let's swear again." So they swore again, with dread solemnities. "I've heard a power of talk, Huck," Tom said.

"It's all Muff Potter, Muff Potter. It keeps me in a sweat."

"I reckon he's a goner. Don't you feel sorry for him sometimes?" Tom asked.

"Most always. He ain't no account, but he ain't ever hurt anybody. He just fishes a little, to get money to get drunk on, and loafs around considerable. But, lord, we all do that. He give me half a fish once, when there warn't enough for two. Lots of times he's kind of stood by me when I was out of luck."

"He's mended kites for me and tied hooks to my line. I wish we could get him out of the jail," Tom said.

"We couldn't get him out. Besides, it wouldn't do any good. They'd ketch 'im again."

"I hate to hear them abuse him so, when he never done it."

"I do, too. I hear them say he's the bloodiest villain in this country and they wonder he wasn't ever hung before."

"Yes, they talk like that all the time. I've heard them say that if he was to get free, they'd lynch him."

"They would, too."

The boys had a long talk, but it brought them little comfort. At twilight they went to the jail and gave Potter some tobacco and matches. His gratitude smote their consciences. They felt cowardly and treacherous to the last degree when Potter said, "You've been mighty good to me, boys—better 'n anybody else. I done an awful thing. I was drunk and crazy at the time; that's the only way I can account for it. Now I got to swing for it, and that's as it should be. Well, we won't talk about that. I don't want to make you feel bad. Stand in the moonlight, so I can see your faces better. It's a prime comfort to see friendly faces when a body's in such a muck of trouble. You're the only ones that come here. Put your hands through the bars so's I can shake 'em. Small hands. But they've helped me a power, and they'd help me more if they could."

Tom went home miserable. His dreams that night were full of horrors. The next day and the day after, he hung around the courtroom, wanting to go in but forcing himself to stay outside. Huck was having the same experience. The boys studiously avoided each other. Tom kept his ears open when idlers sauntered out of the courtroom and invariably heard distressing news. Things looked bad for

Potter. After two days the town talk was that Injun Joe's evidence stood firm and that there was no question as to what the verdict would be.

The next morning, the whole town flocked to the courthouse. After a long wait the jury filed in and took their places. Soon after, Potter—pale, haggard, timid, and hopeless—was brought in, with chains on him, and seated where everyone could stare at him. No less conspicuous was Injun Joe, unmoved as ever. The judge arrived, and the sheriff proclaimed the opening of the court.

A witness testified that he had found Potter washing in the brook at an early hour of the morning on the day the murder was discovered. Potter immediately had sneaked away, he said. Another witness identified the knife found near the corpse. A third witness swore that he had often seen the knife in Potter's possession. Several witnesses commented that Potter had acted guilty when he was brought to the murder scene. Every detail of the damaging circumstances was brought out by credible witnesses.

To the audience's growing disapproval and annoyance, Potter's attorney continually declined to cross-examine anyone. Did this attorney mean to throw away his client's life without an effort?

The prosecution concluded, "By the oaths of citizens whose word is above suspicion, we have fastened this awful crime, beyond all question, on the prisoner. We rest our case." Potter groaned, put his face in his hands, and rocked himself to and fro. The courtroom was silent.

Potter's attorney rose and said, "Your honor, at the opening of this trial, we stated our intention to plead that our client committed this deed while delirious with drink. We have changed our mind and will not offer that plea." Turning to the clerk, the attorney announced, "Call Thomas Sawyer."

Every face in the house, including Potter's, showed amazement. Every eye fastened on Tom as he rose and took his place on the stand. Tom looked as frightened as he felt. The oath was administered.

"Thomas Sawyer, where were you on the seventeenth of June about the hour of midnight?"

Tom glanced at Injun Joe's iron face, and his tongue failed him. The audience waited, breathless. After a few moments, Tom managed to say, "In the graveyard."

"A bit louder, please. Don't be afraid. You were . . ."

"In the graveyard."

A contemptuous smile flitted across Joe's face.

"Were you anywhere near Horse Williams' grave?"

"Yes, sir."

"Speak up, please. How near were you?"

"Near as I am to you."

"Were you hidden?"

"Yes."

"Where?"

"Behind the elms on the edge of the grave."

Joe gave a barely perceptible start.

"Was anyone with you?"

"Yes, sir. I went there with . . ."

"Never mind. You needn't mention your companion's name. We will produce him at the proper time. Did you bring anything to the graveyard"?

Tom hesitated and looked confused.

"Speak up, my boy. The truth always is respectable. What did you bring?"

"A dead cat."

There was a ripple of mirth, which the court silenced. "We will produce that cat's skeleton," the attorney said. "Now, my boy, tell us everything that occurred. Don't leave anything out, and don't be afraid."

Tom began, hesitantly. As he warmed to his subject, his words flowed more easily. With parted lips, the audience hung on every word. Emotion reached its climax when Tom said, "As Dr. Robinson hit Muff Potter with the board and Muff Potter fell, Injun Joe jumped with the knife and..."

Quick as lightning, Joe sprang for a window and was gone.

The fickle world took Muff Potter to its bosom and fondled him as lavishly as it previously had abused him. Once again, Tom was a glittering hero—pet of the old, envy of the young. His name went into immortal print. (The town newspaper reported on his testimony.) Some people believed that he would be President someday, if he escaped hanging.

Each day, Potter's gratitude made Tom glad that he had spoken. But each night, he wished that he had sealed his tongue. Injun Joe appeared in all his dreams, always with doom in his eye. Hardly any temptation could persuade Tom to leave the house after nightfall. Half the time, Tom was afraid that Joe never would be captured; half the time he was afraid that he *would* be. Tom felt sure that he never would draw another safe breath until Joe was dead and he had seen the corpse.

Huck was in the same state of terror because Tom had told the whole story to Potter's attorney the night before the final day of the trial. Huck was afraid that his role in the business might leak out, even though he had been spared testifying in court and Potter's attorney had promised to keep his secret. After all, Tom too had promised to keep the secret but hadn't, so Huck's confidence in the human race was pretty much obliterated.

Rewards had been offered for information on Joe's whereabouts, and the country had been scoured, but Joe had not been found. A real-live detective came up from St. Louis, nosed around, shook his head, looked wise, and found a clue. You can't hang a clue for murder, so when the detective finished and went home, Tom and Huck felt as insecure as before.

Chapter 13

There comes a time in the life of every well-constructed boy when he has a raging desire to go somewhere and dig for hidden treasure. When this desire came over Tom, he looked for Joe Harper but failed to find him. Next he sought Ben Rogers, but Ben had gone fishing. Presently he stumbled upon Huck, who would suffice.

Tom took Huck to a private place and confided the matter. Huck was willing. Huck always was willing to take part in an enterprise that offered entertainment and required no financial investment.

"Where'll we dig?" Huck asked.

"'Most anywhere."

"Why? Is it hid all around?"

"No. It's hid in mighty particular places."

"Who hides it?"

"Why, robbers, of course. Who do you reckon—Sunday school sup'rintendents?"

"I don't know. If it was mine, I wouldn't hide

it. I'd spend it and have a good time."

"So would I. But robbers don't do that. They always hide it and leave it."

"Don't they come after it?"

"No. They think they will, but they generally forget the location, or else they die. Anyway, it lays there a long time and gets rusty. By and by, somebody finds an old yellow paper that tells how to find it."

"Have you got one of them papers?"

"No."

"Then, how will we find it?"

"They always bury treasure on an island, or under the floor of a ha'nted house, or under an old dead tree that's got one limb sticking out. S'pose we try that old dead tree on the hill near the ha'nted house. The combination of an old dead tree *and* a ha'nted house might improve our chances. We might find a brass pot with a hundred dollars in it or a rotted chest full of di'monds."

Huck's eyes glowed. "That's bully. Just gimme the hundred dollars; I don't want no di'monds."

"Alright. *I* ain't gonna throw over no di'monds. Some of 'em's worth twenty dollars apiece."

"Really?"

"Cert'nly. Ain't you ever seen one?"

"Not that I remember."

"Kings have loads of 'em."

"Well, I don' know no kings."

They got a pick and shovel and set out on

their three-mile tramp. They arrived hot and panting and threw themselves down in an elm's shade to rest.

"Say, Huck, if we find a treasure, what you goin' to do with your share?"

"I'll have pie and soda every day, and I'll go to every circus that comes along."

"What you goin' to do with yours, Tom?"

"I'm goin' to buy a new drum, a real sword, and a red necktie, and get married."

"Married! Why, you ain't in your right mind."

"I got someone in particular in mind."

"Really? Who?"

"Never you mind. Let's get digging."

They worked and sweated for half an hour. No result. They toiled another half hour. Still no result. "Do they always bury it this deep?" Huck asked.

"Not generally. I reckon we haven't got the right place."

They chose a new spot and began again. They dug in silence for some time. Finally Huck leaned on his shovel, wiped the sweat from his brow with his sleeve, and asked, "Where we goin' t' dig next, after we get *this* treasure?"

"Maybe we'll tackle the old tree on Cardiff Hill, behind the widow's."

"Won't the widow take the treasure away from us if it's on her land?"

"Whoever finds a hid treasure gets to keep it.

It don't make any difference whose land it's on."

That was satisfactory. The work continued for a time. Then Huck said, "Blame it, we must be in the wrong place again. What do you think?"

"I don't understand it. Sometimes witches interfere. Maybe that's what's happened."

"Witches ain't got no power in the daytime."

"That's true. Oh, *I* know what's the matter. We've got to find out where the limb's shadow falls at midnight. That's where we need to dig. We've got to do it tonight because if somebody sees these holes, they'll know there's treasure somewhere around here, and they'll get it before we do."

"I'll come around tonight and meow."

"Alright. Let's hide the tools in the bushes."

The boys returned that night. They sat in shadow, waiting. It was a lonely place. Spirits whispered in the rustling leaves, and ghosts lurked in the murky nooks. When they judged that midnight had come, they marked where the limb's shadow fell and began to dig. The hole got deeper and deeper. Every time the pick struck something, they felt a surge of excitement. But every time it was only a stone or chunk.

At last Tom said, "It ain't any use, Huck. We're wrong again."

"We *can't* be wrong," Huck protested. "We spotted the shadow to a dot."

"I know, but we weren't sure it was midnight; we only guessed. It must've been before or after midnight, not right *at* midnight."

Huck dropped his shovel. "We got to give this up. We can't ever tell the time exac'ly. Besides, there's too many witches and ghosts flutterin' around here. I been creepin' all over since I got here."

"Me, too. They 'most always put in a dead man when they bury a treasure under a tree, to guard it."

"Lordy, Tom! I don't like to fool around much where there's dead people. A body's bound to get into trouble with 'em."

"S'pose this one here was to stick his skull out and say something!"

"Don't, Tom! It's awful. Let's try somewheres else."

"Alright. I reckon we better. Let's try the ha'nted house."

"Blame it, I don't like ha'nted houses. Why, ghosts are worse'n dead people. They come slidin' around in a shroud when you ain't noticin' and peep over your shoulder all of a sudden. I couldn't stand such a thing."

"Well, ghosts don't travel around in the day-time. They won't interfere with us digging there during the day."

"Well, alright. We'll tackle the ha'nted house if you say so, but I reckon it's takin' chances."

They had started down the hill. There, in the middle of the moonlit valley below, stood the haunted house, utterly isolated, its fences gone long ago, weeds smothering its doorstep, its chimney crumbled to ruins, a corner of its roof caved in. The boys gazed awhile, then headed off far to the right (to give the haunted house a wide berth) and went home through the woods.

Around noon the next day, the boys arrived at the dead tree. They had come for their tools. Tom was impatient to go to the haunted house. Huck was less eager. Then he remembered that it was Friday and informed Tom of this ominous fact.

"I never once thought of it, Huck."

"Me neither, but all at once it popped into my mind."

"We might've got into an awful scrape tackling such a thing on a Friday."

"That's for sure. This is risky enough without some bad-luck day."

"We'll drop this thing for today."

And they did.

On Saturday, shortly after noon, the boys were at the dead tree again. Shouldering their tools, they headed to the haunted house. When they reached it, they crept to the door and fearfully peeped in. They saw an unplastered room with no floor, an ancient fireplace, vacant windows, a ruinous staircase, and, all around, cobwebs. They entered softly, with quickened pulses, talking in whispers, ears alert to the slightest sound, muscles tense and ready for instant retreat. Familiarity soon lessened their fear, and they gave the place a critical and interested examination while admiring their own boldness. Next they wanted to look upstairs. This was something like cutting off retreat, but they dared each other, so they put their tools in a corner and made the ascent. Upstairs were the same signs of decay. Tom and Huck were about to go down and begin work when Tom whispered, "Sh!"

"What is it?" Huck whispered.

"Sh! Hear it?"

"Yes! Let's run."

"Keep still! They're coming toward the door."

The boys stretched themselves on the floor, with their eyes to knotholes in the planking, and fearfully waited.

Two men entered. Each boy thought, "It's the old Mexican that's been in town once or twice lately. Never saw the other man before."

The Mexican wore a poncho, a sombrero, and a patch over one eye; he had long white hair and bushy white whiskers. The other man was younger, ragged and unkempt, with an unpleasant face. He talked in a low voice. The two sat on the ground, facing the door, with their backs to the wall.

"No," the younger man said. "I've thought it over, and I don't like it. It's dangerous."

"Dangerous! Don't be such a milksop, Griggs." The voice made the boys gasp. It was Injun Joe's! "That job up yonder was dangerous, and nothing came of it."

"That was different—way up the river and not another house around," Griggs said.

"We shouldn't 've come here in the daytime," Joe said. "Anybody who saw us would be suspicious."

"I know, but there warn't any other place as handy after that fool job. I want to quit this shanty. I wanted to yesterday, only it warn't any use trying to leave here with those infernal boys playing right there on the hill."

The "infernal boys" quaked and felt lucky that they had remembered it was Friday and had decided to wait a day. They wished they had waited a year.

The two men got out some food and ate. After a long silence, Joe said, "Listen. Go back up the river where you belong. Wait there 'til you hear from me. I'll risk dropping into town one more time. We'll do the job after I've looked around a little and think things look alright for it. Then we'll head to Texas. Now, I'm dead for sleep. It's your turn to watch." Joe lay down and soon was asleep. Griggs soon began to nod. His head drooped lower and lower. Then he, too, was asleep.

The boys drew a long, grateful breath. Tom whispered, "Now's our chance. Come on."

"I can't. I'd die if they woke up."

Tom urged.

Huck refused.

So, rising slowly and softly, Tom started alone.

His first step made the floor creak so badly that he sank down almost dead with fright. The boys lay there for what seemed eternity. The sun was setting. Joe sat up, looked around, stirred Griggs with his foot, and said, "You're some watchman. Nearly time for us to be moving. What'll we do with the silver?"

"Leave it here, I reckon," Griggs said. "No use taking it 'til we start south.

"Alright, but I think we'd better bury it."

"Good idea." Griggs walked across the room, knelt down, raised a hearth stone, and took out a bag that jingled pleasantly. He subtracted about twenty dollars from it for himself and as much for Joe. He passed the bag to Joe, who was on his knees in the corner, digging with his knife.

The boys had forgotten all their fears. With wide eyes they watched every movement; a bag of silver was treasure in the happiest circumstances, those that required no guessing about where to dig. Tom and Huck repeatedly gave each other nudges that communicated, "Ain't you glad *now* that we're here!"

Joe's knife struck something.

"What is it?" Griggs asked.

"Half-rotten plank. No, it's a box. Give me a hand, and we'll see what's in it. Never mind; I've broke a hole." Joe reached in. "Man, it's money!"

The two men examined the handful of coins. They were gold. The boys above were as excited as the two men.

Griggs said, "We'll make quick work of this. There's an old, rusty pick in the corner by the fire-place. I saw it a minute ago." He ran and got the boys' pick and shovel.

Joe took the pick, looked it over, shook his head, muttered something to himself, and then began to use it. The box soon was unearthed. The men contemplated the treasure in blissful silence.

"Partner, there's thousands of dollars here," Joe said.

"It always was said that Murrel's gang used to be around here."

"This must be their loot," Joe said.

"Now you won't need to do that job."

Joe frowned. "It ain't just money I want. It's revenge." A light flamed in his eyes. "I'll need your help in it. When it's finished, then Texas. Go home, and stand by 'til you hear from me."

"If you say so. What'll we do with this? Bury it again?"

"Yes. [Joy overhead.] No! [Distress overhead.] That pick had fresh earth on it. [Terror overhead.] What's a pick and shovel doin' here? Who brought them, and where did they go? If we bury it again, they'll see the ground was disturbed and have a look. We'll take it to my den."

"Number One?" Griggs asked.

"No, Number Two, under the cross." Joe went from window to window, cautiously looking out.

"Who could have brought those tools here? Do you reckon they can be upstairs?"

The boys' breath stopped. Joe put his hand on his knife and turned toward the stairway. His steps came creaking up the stairs. The boys were about to leap for a closet when there was a crash of rotten boards and Joe landed on the ground amid the rubble of the collapsed stairway. He gathered himself up, cursing.

The two men got ready to leave. In the twilight, they slipped out of the house and moved toward the river with their precious box.

Tom and Huck got up, weak but vastly relieved. Through the chinks between the house's logs, they stared after the departing men. They managed to get back downstairs without breaking their necks. As they headed toward town, they didn't talk much. They were too busy hating themselves and the ill luck that had made them leave the pick and shovel where Joe could see them. They resolved to keep a lookout for Joe when he came to town and follow him to Number Two, wherever that might be.

Then a ghastly thought occurred to Tom. "Revenge. What if he means *us*, Huck?"

Huck nearly fainted.

They talked it over. Joe might mean somebody else, they agreed. Or he might mean only Tom because only Tom had testified. The thought of being alone in danger offered Tom no comfort.

When it came to being in danger, he preferred company.

The day's adventure tormented Tom's dreams that night. Four times Tom had his hands on the treasure; four times it vanished as he awoke.

In the morning Tom hurriedly ate breakfast and went to find Huck. He found Huck sitting on a flatboat dangling his feet in the water and looking glum.

"Hello, Huck."

"Hello." Pause. "Tom, if we'd left the blame tools at the dead tree, we'd 've got the money."

"There's only one thing to do—find Injun Joe."

"We'll never find him. A feller has only one chance for such a pile, and that one's lost. Anyway, I'd feel mighty shaky if I was to see him again."

"So would I, but I want to track him to his Number Two."

"Yes, Number Two. What do you reckon it is?"

"I don' know. Maybe it's the number of a house."

"If it is, it ain't in this town. There ain't no house numbers here."

"That's so. Lemme think a minute. Maybe it's the number of a room in an inn."

"Might be! They ain't only two inns, so we can find out quick."

"Stay here, Huck, 'til I come."

Tom was off at once. He did not care to have

Huck's company in public places. He returned in half an hour and told Huck what he had learned. In the better inn, Room Two had long been occupied by a young lawyer and was still so occupied. In the less expensive inn, Room Two was a mystery. The innkeeper's young son said it was locked all the time, and he never saw anyone go into it or come out of it except at night. He had noticed a light in it last night. "I reckon that's the room we're after, Huck."

"I reckon it is. What should we do?"

Tom thought a long time, then said, "The back door of Room Two is on that little alley between the inn and the old brick store. Get hold of all the door keys that you can find, and I'll get hold of Auntie's. The first dark night, we'll go there and try 'em. Mind you, keep a lookout for Injun Joe. He said he was gonna drop into town and spy around once more for a chance to get revenge. If you see him, follow him. If he don't go to Room Two, that ain't the place."

"Lordy, I don't want to foller him by myself!"

"It'll be night. He might never see you. And if he did, he might not think anything of it."

"Well, if it's really dark, I reckon I can track him. I'll try."

That night Tom and Huck hung around the area of the inn until after nine. One watched the alley, the other the inn door. Nobody entered or left the alley. Nobody resembling Injun Joe entered

or left the inn. Tom went home with the understanding that if it became really dark, Huck would
come and meow; then Tom would slip out and try
the keys. But the night remained moonlit and
clear, so Huck ended his watch and went to bed in
an empty sugar barrel around midnight.

Tuesday and Wednesday the boys had the
same ill luck. But Thursday night Tom slipped out
with his aunt's lantern and a large towel to cover it
with. He hid the lantern in Huck's sugar barrel,
and the watch began. An hour before midnight the
inn closed and its lights went out. The darkness
was black; the stillness was interrupted only by
occasional rumblings of distant thunder. Inside the
barrel, Tom lit the lantern and wrapped it in the
towel. The two adventurers crept toward the inn.
Huck stood sentry as Tom felt his way into the
alley. The longer Tom was gone, the more fearful
Huck became. It seemed that hours had passed.
Tom must have fainted, Huck thought. Maybe he
was dead. Maybe his heart had burst with terror.
Huck fearfully approached the alley. There was a
sudden flash of light, and Tom came tearing by.
"Run!" he cried. "Run for your life!"

He needn't have repeated it. Huck was traveling
at about thirty miles an hour before the repetition
occurred.

The boys didn't stop until they reached a
deserted slaughterhouse at the town's lower end.
Just as they got inside, the storm burst and rain

poured down. As soon as Tom got his breath, he said, "Huck, it was awful. I tried two of the keys as soft as I could, but they made such a racket, I was scared to death. They wouldn't turn in the lock, either. Without noticing what I was doing, I took hold of the knob and the door opened. It warn't locked. I hopped in and shook off the towel, and—great Caesar's ghost—I 'most stepped onto Injun Joe's hand!"

"No!"

"Yes! He was lying there, sound asleep on the floor, with his patch on his eye and his arms spread out."

"Lordy, what did you do? Did he wake up?"

"No, never budged. Drunk, I reckon. I grabbed that towel and ran."

"I'd never've thought of the towel."

"Well, *I* did. My aunt would make me mighty sick if I lost it."

"Did you see the box?"

"I didn't wait to look around. I didn't see anything but a bottle and a tin cup on the floor by Injun Joe, and lots more bottles in the room."

"Say, Tom, now's a mighty good time to get the box, if Injun Joe's drunk."

"*You* try it!"

Huck shuddered. "No, I reckon not."

After a long pause, Tom said, "Let's not try anymore 'til we know Injun Joe's not in there. If we watch every night, we'll be sure to see him go out.

Then we'll snatch the box."

"I'm agreed. I'll watch the whole night, and I'll do it every night, if you'll do the other part of the job."

"Alright. All you got to do is come and meow. If I'm asleep, throw some gravel at the window. That'll fetch me. Where will you sleep during the day?" Tom asked.

"Ben Rogers' hayloft. He lets me. So does his pap's Negro man, Uncle Jake. I tote water for Uncle Jake whenever he wants me to, and any time I ask him, he gives me a little somethin' to eat if he can spare it. That's a mighty good Negro, Tom. He likes me 'cause I don't ever act as if I was above him. Sometimes I've set right down and ate *with* him. But don't tell nobody that. A body's got to do things when he's awful hungry that he wouldn't do as a steady thing."

Chapter 14

The first thing that Tom heard on Friday morning was a glad piece of news: Becky had returned to town the night before. Injun Joe and the treasure dropped to secondary importance. Tom saw Becky, and they had an exhausting good time playing with a crowd of schoolmates. Also, Becky's long-anticipated picnic would take place the next day. The news threw the town's young people into a fever of anticipation.

By ten the next morning, a rollicking company was gathered at Becky's house. It was not the custom for elderly people to mar children's picnics with their presence. The children were considered safe enough under the wings of a few ladies and gentlemen of twenty or so years.

The steam ferryboat had been chartered for the occasion. Bessie Thatcher said to Becky, "You won't get back 'til late. Maybe you'd better stay all night with one of the girls who live near the ferry landing."

"I'll stay with Susie Harper, Mamma."

"Good. Behave yourself, and don't be any trouble."

Presently the merry crowd filed up the main street with baskets of provisions. As they tripped along, Tom said to Becky, "Instead of going to the Harpers' tonight, let's climb the hill and visit Widow Douglas. She's sure to give us some ice cream." Becky agreed.

Presently it occurred to Tom that Huck might come this very night and give the meow signal. But the certain fun of having ice cream outweighed the uncertain treasure. Tom yielded to the stronger temptation and pushed the box of money from his mind.

Three miles below town the ferry stopped at the mouth of a woody hollow. The crowd swarmed ashore. Soon the forest and craggy heights echoed with shouts and laughter. The children worked through all the different ways of getting hot and tired. Then they straggled back to camp with huge appetites. After the feast there was a refreshing rest and chat in the shade of spreading oaks.

By and by, somebody shouted, "Who's ready for the cave?"

Everyone was. The children grabbed candles and scampered up the hill containing McDougal's Cave. The cave's massive oak door stood unbarred. Within was a small chamber, chilly as an icehouse. The limestone walls were dewy with a cold sweat.

It was romantic and mysterious to stand in the cave's deep gloom and look out over the green valley shining in the sun.

After some romping, the procession filed deeper into the cave, down a narrow, steeply descending path. Their candlelight dimly revealed lofty walls of rock and branching crevices. The cave was a vast maze of crooked aisles. It was said that a person could wander for days through the cave's tangle of chasms and never find the end. No one *knew* the cave. Most of the young men knew part of it, and it was customary not to venture much beyond that part. Tom knew as much of the cave as anyone.

The procession moved about three-quarters of a mile down the cave's main avenue. Then groups and couples began to slip aside into branch avenues, fly along the dark corridors, and take each other by surprise where the corridors came together again. By twilight one group after another straggled back to the cave's mouth—panting, dirty with candle drippings, and entirely happy. They were astonished to find that night was at hand. The ferry's bell was clanging that all passengers should return. With the picnickers back on board, it started off.

Huck was keeping watch when the ferry's lights glinted past the wharf. The night was growing cloudy and dark.

Ten o'clock came. The noise of vehicles ceased,

scattered lights winked out, all stragglers disappeared, and the town slept, leaving Huck alone with the silence.

Eleven o'clock came, and the inn lights went out. Darkness was everywhere now.

Huck waited a weary long time. Then he heard a noise. Instantly he was all attention. The alley door closed softly. Huck sprang to the corner of the brick store. The next moment two men brushed by him. One had something under his arm. It must be the box! They were going to remove the treasure. It was pointless to go for Tom: the men would get away with the box. Huck decided to follow them. He stepped out and glided along behind the men—cat-like, with bare feet, allowing them to keep just far enough ahead to be visible.

The men went down various streets and up Cardiff Hill. After the summit they plunged into a narrow path between tall bushes and were immediately hidden in the gloom. Huck shortened his following distance. He stopped, listened, and heard nothing. Heavens, was everything lost? Suddenly a man cleared his throat not four feet from him. Huck felt his heart shoot into his throat. He knew where he was: Caroline Douglas's house.

Injun Joe spoke in a low voice. "Damn her. Maybe she's got company, There's lights on."

"Yes, there must be company there. Better give

it up." It was Griggs.

Huck felt a deadly chill. This, then, was the revenge job. His first thought was to flee. Then he remembered that Caroline Douglas had been kind to him more than once. Maybe these men were going to murder her! He wanted to warn her, but he didn't dare move.

"Give it up?" Joe responded. "I might never get another chance. Her husband was rough on me, many times. He was the justice of the peace that jailed me for a vagrant. And that ain't all. It ain't a millionth of it. He had me whipped—in front of the jail, with the whole town looking on. He's dead, but I can take it out on *her*."

"Oh, don't kill her!" Griggs said.

"Who said anything about killing? I'd kill *him* if he was here, but not her. When you want revenge on a woman, you don't kill her; you go for her looks. You slit her nostrils and notch her ears."

"My God, that's . . ."

"Keep your opinion to yourself. You'll help me do this. If you flinch, I'll kill you. And if I have to kill you, I'll also have to kill her. We'll go in when the lights are out."

Holding his breath, Huck stepped back cautiously—first one foot, then the other. Again he stepped back. A twig snapped under his foot! His breath stopped, and he listened. Silence. His gratitude was measureless. As carefully as if he were a ship, he turned in his tracks. Then he stepped along quickly but cautiously. Soon he felt secure and started to run. Down, down he sped.

At the first house, Huck banged on the door.

Hugh Jones and his two grown sons thrust their heads out the windows. "Who's banging? What do you want?" Jones asked.

"Let me in! Quick!"

"Who are you?"

"Huckleberry Finn. Quick! Let me in!"

"Let him in, lads. Let's see what's the trouble."

"Please don't ever tell that I told you," Huck said as soon as he was inside. "I'd be killed, for sure. But the widow's been good to me. I'll tell if you promise you won't ever say it was me."

"Out with it, lad," Jones said. "Nobody here'll tell."

Three minutes later Jones and his sons—well armed—were up the hill and approaching Caroline Douglas's house. Huck accompanied them no farther. He hid behind a boulder and listened. There was an anxious silence, then an explosion of firearms and a cry. Huck sped down the hill as fast as his legs could carry him.

Before dawn on Sunday, Huck went up the hill and gently knocked on Jones's door. The knocking woke the residents. A call came from a window: "Who's there?"

"Huck Finn. Please let me in."

"It's a name that can open this door day or night, lad. Welcome."

These were strange, pleasant words to the homeless boy's ears. The door was quickly unlocked, and Huck entered. He was given a seat. Jones and his tall sons quickly dressed.

"Now, my boy, I hope you're good and hungry because breakfast will be ready as soon as the sun's up. The boys and I hoped you'd turn up here last night."

"I was awful scared," Huck said, "so I run. I've come now 'cause I wanted to know about it. Are they dead?"

"No, they ain't dead, I'm sorry to say. We crept along on tiptoe 'til we got within fifteen feet of them. It was dark as a cellar. I was in the lead, with my pistol raised, and then I sneezed! Couldn't hold it back. When I sneezed, those scoundrels moved. I called out, 'Fire, boys!' and shot at the place where the noise came from. So did the boys. Those villains were off in a jiffy, down through the woods, with us after them. I think we never touched them. They fired a shot apiece as they started, but their bullets whizzed by and didn't do us any harm. As soon as we lost the sound of their feet, we quit chasing. We went down and woke the law officers. They got a posse together and went off to guard the riverbank. As soon as it's light, the sheriff and a gang will search the woods. I wish we had some sort of description of those rascals. It'd help a lot. Can you describe them at all?"

"Yes. I saw them in town and follered them."

"Splendid! Describe them, my boy."

"One's a mean-looking, raggedy guy named Griggs. The other's . . . The other's Injun Joe! He's dressed like a Mexican, with long white hair and whiskers, a Mexican cape and hat, and a patch over one eye."

"Off with you, boys. Tell the sheriff." Jones's sons departed at once.

During breakfast Huck felt that everything was drifting in the right direction. The treasure must still be in Room Two. Injun Joe and Griggs would be captured and jailed. Then he and Tom could seize the gold without any fear of interruption.

As breakfast ended, there was a knock at the door. Huck jumped for a hiding place. Jones admitted several ladies and gentlemen, among them Caroline Douglas. Jones told the visitors the story of the night before. The widow expressed deep gratitude.

"Don't say a word about it, ma'am."

"I went to sleep reading in bed and slept through all that noise," Caroline Douglas said. "Why didn't you come and wake me?"

"We judged it warn't worthwhile. Those fellows warn't likely to come again. What was the use of waking you and scaring you to death? My three Negro men stood guard at your house all the rest of the night."

The news spread, and more visitors came.

Poor Jones had to tell and retell the story a couple of hours more.

There was no Sunday school during vacation, but everyone was at church early. So far, there was no sign of the two villains. When the sermon ended, Bessie Thatcher went up to Sereny Harper and said, "Is my Becky going to sleep all day? I guess she's all tired out."

"Becky?"

Bessie Thatcher looked startled. "Yes. Didn't she stay with you last night?"

"Why, no."

Bessie Thatcher turned pale and sank into a pew, just as Aunt Polly passed by.

"Good morning, Bessie," Aunt Polly said. "Good morning, Sereny. Tom's turned up missing. I reckon he stayed at one of your houses last night, and now he's afraid to come to church."

Bessie Thatcher shook her head weakly and turned paler.

"Tom didn't stay with us," Sereny Harper said, beginning to look uneasy.

A marked anxiety came into Aunt Polly's face. "Joe Harper, have you seen Tom this morning?"

"No, ma'am."

"When did you see him last?"

Joe tried to remember but wasn't sure.

The people had stopped moving out of the church. Whispers passed along, and a growing uneasiness appeared on every face. Children were anxiously questioned, and young teachers. They all said that they had not noticed whether Tom and Becky were on board the ferry on the homeward trip. It had been dark, and no one had thought to ask if anyone was missing.

One young man finally blurted out his fear that they were still in the cave. Bessie Thatcher fainted. Aunt Polly started crying and wringing her hands. The alarm spread. Within five minutes the bells were clanging wildly and the whole town was up. The Cardiff Hill episode instantly sank into insignificance. Horses were saddled, skiffs were manned, the ferry was ordered out, and before the horror was half an hour old, two hundred men were pouring down the road and river toward the cave.

Throughout the afternoon many women visited Aunt Polly and Bessie Thatcher, trying to comfort them. They cried with them—which was better than words.

Throughout the night the town waited for news. But when dawn came, the only word was, "Send food and more candles." Bessie Thatcher and Aunt Polly were almost crazed.

Hugh Jones came home toward daylight, spattered with candle grease and almost worn out. He found Huck still in the bed that had been provided for him—delirious with fever. The physicians were all at the cave, so Caroline Douglas came to look after the patient.

By late morning exhausted men began to straggle into the town, but the strongest men continued searching. Parts of the cave were being searched that never had been visited before. Candlelight flitted through every nook and crevice. Shouts and pistol shots echoed down the somber aisles.

In one place, far from the section usually traveled by tourists, "Becky and Tom" had been found written on the rocky wall with candle smoke. Nearby the searchers had found a bit of ribbon. Bessie Thatcher recognized the ribbon as Becky's and cried over it.

Three dreadful days and nights dragged along. The town sank into a hopeless stupor.

Chapter 15

Let's return now to Tom and Becky at the picnic. They traveled the cave's aisles with the rest of the company. When hide-and-seek play began, Tom and Becky engaged in it with zeal. When they tired of that, they wandered down a winding avenue holding their candles aloft and reading the tangle of names, dates, addresses, and statements with which the rocky walls had been marked in candle smoke. Drifting along and talking, they scarcely noticed when they reached a part of the cave with unmarked walls. They smoked their own names and moved on. Presently they came to a little stream that trickled over a ledge of gleaming stone. Tom squeezed behind the small waterfall so that he could illuminate it for Becky's gratification. He found that it curtained a steep, narrow natural stairway. The ambition to be a discoverer seized him. Becky responded to his call. They made a smoke mark for future guidance and started on their quest.

They wound their way down into the cave's depths, made another mark, and branched off in search of novelties. They found a spacious cavern from whose ceiling hung many shining stalactites as long and thick as a man's leg. They left the cavern by way of a passage that brought them to another cavern, with numerous fantastic pillars formed by the joining of stalactites and stalagmites. In the midst of the cave was a spring whose basin was encrusted with glittering crystals. Under the roof were thousands of bats. The candlelight disturbed them, causing them to come flocking down, squeaking and darting. Seizing her hand, Tom hurried Becky into a corridor, but not before a bat struck out Becky's candle with his wing.

Tom and Becky soon discovered a subterranean lake that stretched dimly until it was lost in shadows. They sat down to rest. Now, for the first time, they became aware of the deep stillness, which laid a clammy hand on their spirits.

"It seems like a long time since I heard any of the others," Becky said.

"I guess we're quite a way below them."

"I wonder how long we've been down here, Tom. I think we'd better start back."

"Yes, I reckon we'd better."

"Can you find the way? It's all a mixed-up crookedness to me."

"Yes, but I think we'd better avoid the bats. If they put our candles out, we'll be in trouble. Let's try some other route."

"I hope we won't get lost. It would be awful." Becky shuddered at the thought.

Tom and Becky started through a corridor and traveled it in silence a long way, glancing at each new opening to see if anything looked familiar. Nothing did. Shaken, Tom started turning off into diverging avenues at random, in the hope of finding the way back. "Oh, Tom, never mind the bats," Becky said. "Let's go back that way."

Tom shouted. The call went echoing down the empty aisles and died out in the distance in a faint sound that resembled a ripple of mocking laughter.

"Don't do it again, Tom. It's horrid."

"It *is* horrid, but I'd better, Becky. They might hear us." He shouted again.

The children stood and listened. Nothing. Tom quickly turned around and headed back, but the indecision of his manner soon revealed a fearful fact: he could not find the way back.

"Oh, Tom, you didn't make any marks."

"I was a fool, Becky. I can't find the way. It's all mixed up."

"We're lost! Oh, why did we ever leave the others?" Becky sank to the ground and started to cry. Tom sat down by her and put his arms around her. She buried her face in his chest and clung to him. Tom begged her to pluck up hope. She said she would try.

They moved on, aimlessly, hand in hand. After

some time, Tom said that they should listen for dripping water, which would indicate a spring. They found one and rested. With some clay, Tom fastened his candle to the wall in front of them.

"I'm so hungry," Becky said.

Tom took something out of his pocket. "Do you remember this?"

Becky almost smiled. "It's our wedding cake."

"Yes, I wish it was as big as a barrel because it's all we've got."

Tom divided the cake, and Becky eagerly ate her portion. Tom nibbled at his. There was abundant cold water to quench their thirst. Becky suggested that they move on, but Tom said, "No, Becky. We have to stay here, where there's water to drink. That little piece is our last candle."

Becky paled, but then brightened. "Tom, they'll miss us and hunt for us! Maybe they're hunting for us now."

"Maybe they are. I hope they are."

"When do you think they'll miss us?"

"When they get back to the boat, I reckon."

"It might be dark then. Would they notice that we didn't come?"

"I don't know. But your mother would miss you as soon as they got home."

The frightened look on Becky's face reminded Tom that Becky was not expected home that night. Sunday morning might be half gone before her mother discovered that she was not with the

Harpers.

The children fastened their eyes on their bit of candle and watched it melt slowly away. At last the half-inch wick stood alone. They saw the feeble flame rise and fall, climb the thin column of smoke, linger at its top a moment, and then . . . utter darkness.

They alternately slept and suffered. Tom said it might be Sunday now, or even Monday. Becky was silent. Tom said that they must have been missed by now and that the search must be underway. He would shout; maybe someone would come. He shouted once. The distant echoes sounded so hideously that he stopped. The hours wasted away, and hunger returned. They split what remained of Tom's cake but only felt hungrier than before.

Then Tom said, "Did you hear that?"

Both held their breath and listened. There was a sound like a far-off shout. Instantly Tom answered it. Leading Becky by the hand, he started groping toward it. He listened again and heard the sound again, apparently a little nearer. "It's them!" Tom exclaimed. "They're coming for us! We're alright now, Becky." The prisoners' joy was almost overwhelming. Their progress was slow, however, because there were many unexpected holes. They soon came to one and had to stop. It might be three feet deep; it might be a hundred. Tom lay on his chest and reached down as far as he could. No bottom. They must stay there and wait until the searchers came. They listened. The shouts were growing more distant! A moment or two more and they were gone. Tom yelled until he was hoarse, but no one responded.

The children groped their way back to the spring. Now Tom had an idea. There were some side passages close at hand. It would be better to explore some of them than pass the time in idleness. Tom took a kite line from his pocket and tied it to a projection of rock, and he and Becky started, Tom in the lead, unwinding the line as he groped along. The corridor ended in an overhang. Tom got down on his knees and felt below, then as far around the corner as he could reach. He made an effort to stretch his hand a little farther to the right. At that moment, a hand holding a candle appeared from behind a rock. Tom shouted with joy. But the person who emerged was Injun Joe! Tom was paralyzed. Much to his surprise, Joe disappeared from sight. Tom wondered why Joe hadn't recognized his voice and come over and killed him for testifying in court. Tom reasoned that the echoes must have disguised his voice. Weak with fright, Tom returned to Becky. He was careful not to reveal that he had seen Joe. Instead he told her that he had shouted in case anyone might hear.

The children waited, then slept again. They awoke with a raging hunger. Becky was very weak and refused to budge. She told Tom to go with the kite line and explore if he chose, but to please return every little while and speak to her. Tom kissed her, with a choking sensation in his throat, and pretended to be confident that they would be found or would find their way out. He took the kite line in his hand and went groping down one of the passages on his hands and knees.

Chapter 16

When Tuesday twilight came, the town of St. Petersburg still mourned. The lost children had not been found. Public prayers had been offered up for them, and many private ones. Most of the searchers had given up and returned to their daily responsibilities. Bessie Thatcher was very ill, often delirious. She would call Becky's name, raise her head and listen, then wearily lay her head back down, with a moan. Aunt Polly had fallen into a deep melancholy; her hair had gone from mostly gray to mostly white. Tuesday night the town went to bed in sorrow.

In the middle of the night, the town's bells started pealing. In a moment the streets were swarming with half-clad people, who shouted, "They've been found! They've been found!" Tin pans and horns were added to the din. Massing together, the population moved toward the river. Tom and Becky were coming in an open carriage. Shouting citizens crowded around it and joined its homeward march, shouting "Hurrah! Hurrah!"

The town was illuminated. No one returned to bed. For half an hour, a procession of townspeople filed through the Thatchers' house. They seized the saved ones and kissed them, squeezed Bessie Thatcher's hand, tried to speak but couldn't, and drifted out raining tears of joy.

Aunt Polly's happiness was complete. Bessie Thatcher's would be complete as soon as Judge Thatcher, still searching at the cave, received the good news from a messenger.

Tom lay on a sofa with an eager audience all around him. He told the history of the wonderful adventure, with many embellishments. He told how he left Becky and went to search for a way out. He went down three avenues, as far as his kite line would reach, and was about to turn back when he glimpsed a far-off speck of light. He dropped the line and groped toward it, pushed his head and shoulders through a small hole, and saw the broad Mississippi! He went back for Becky and led her to the blue speck of daylight. He pushed his way out and helped her out. They both sat and cried for joy. Some men came along in a skiff. Tom hailed them and explained the situation. At first, the men didn't believe him because he and Becky were five miles below the valley with the cave. The men took them aboard, rowed to a house, gave them supper, made them rest until several hours after dark, then brought them home.

Before dawn Judge Thatcher and the handful of searchers with him were found and informed of the great news.

Three days of toil and hunger in the cave were not to be shaken off at once, as Tom and Becky soon discovered. They were bedridden Wednesday and Thursday and seemed to grow increasingly tired. Tom got around a little on Thursday, was downtown on Friday, and was almost like new on Saturday. Becky did not leave her room until Sunday, and then she looked as if she had passed through a wasting illness.

Tom learned that Huck was ill and went to see him. Tom was told not to excite Huck with the story of his adventure, and Caroline Douglas stayed by to see that he obeyed.

At home Tom learned of the Cardiff Hill event. He also learned that Griggs's body had been found in the river near the ferry landing. Apparently, Griggs had drowned while fleeing from Hugh Jones and his sons.

About two weeks after his rescue from the cave, Tom started off to visit Huck, who now was strong enough for exciting talk. On the way, Tom stopped to visit Becky. Judge Thatcher jokingly asked Tom if he would like to go to the cave again. To the judge's surprise, Tom answered, "I wouldn't mind it."

"Well, that won't be possible, Tom. So that no one else will ever get lost in that cave, I had its door triple-locked. I've got the keys."

Tom turned white. "Oh, Judge! Injun Joe's in the cave!"

Within a few minutes the news had spread and a dozen skiffs loaded with men were on their way to McDougal's Cave. Filled with passengers, the ferry soon followed. Tom was in the skiff that bore Judge Thatcher.

When the cave door was unlocked, a horrid sight presented itself. Injun Joe lay stretched on the ground, dead. His face was close to the door's crack, as if his longing eyes had been fixed, to the last moment, on the light and cheer of the free world outside. Tom felt pity; he knew, from his own experience, how Joe must have suffered. But he also felt great relief.

Ordinarily there were half a dozen bits of candle (left by tourists) stuck around in the crevices of the entry area, but there were none now. Joe had eaten them. He also had eaten a few bats, leaving only their claws. Nearby was a stone in which Joe had scooped a shallow hollow. He had placed this stone under a stalactite, to catch each precious drop of water that dripped every three minutes, a spoonful in twenty-four hours.

Joe was buried near the cave's mouth. People flocked to the funeral in boats and wagons from towns and farms seven miles around. They brought their children and all sorts of provisions. They had almost as good a time as they would have had at Joe's hanging.

The morning after the funeral, Tom took Huck to a private place for an important talk. By this time Huck had learned all about Tom's adventure from Hugh Jones and Caroline Douglas. Huck now told Tom about *his*. He revealed that he had followed Joe to Caroline Douglas's house. "But you keep mum," Huck said. "I reckon Injun Joe's left friends behind. I don't want 'em goin' after me out o' revenge. If it hadn't been for me, he'd be down in Texas now." Huck paused. "What about the treasure, Tom? Somebody else must've got it by now."

"That's the main thing I wanted to talk you about. I jus' thought I'd lead up to it, so it would get the emphasis that it deserves. The treasure's in McDougal's Cave!"

"What? Isn't it in Number Two?"

"If it ever was there, it ain't there now. It's in the cave. Will you go in there with me and help get it out?"

"You bet I will! That is, I will if it's where we can find our way and not get lost."

"We can do it without the least bit of trouble."

Huck was thrilled. "When do you want to do it, then?"

"Right now, if you're strong enough."

"Is it far inside the cave? I been up and about three days now, but I can't walk more 'n a mile or so—least, I don't think I can."

"It's about five miles into the cave the way anybody but me would go, but there's a mighty shortcut that nobody but me knows about. I'll take you right to it in a skiff."

"Let's start right off!"

"We need some bread and meat, two sacks, two or three kite strings, and some matches."

Shortly after noon the boys "borrowed" a skiff from someone who was absent and set out. When they were several miles below the valley of McDougal's Cave, Tom said, "See that white place up yonder where there's been a landslide? That's one of my marks. Let's get ashore now." They landed.

"Now, Huck, where we're standin' you could take a fishing pole and touch that hole I got out of. See if you can find it." Huck searched all around the place and found nothing. Tom proudly marched into a thick clump of bushes and said, "Here you are! Look at it, Huck—the snuggest hole in this country. You keep mum about it. All along I've been wanting to be a robber, but I knew I had to have a thing like this. We've got it now, and we'll keep it quiet. We'll let only Joe Harper and Ben Rogers know because, of course, there's got to be a gang or else there wouldn't be any style about it. Tom Sawyer's Gang. Don't that sound splendid, Huck?"

"It does, Tom. Who'll we rob?"

"Oh, most anybody."

"And kill them?"

"No, not always. Keep them in the cave 'til they raise a ransom."

"What's a ransom?"

"Money. You make them raise all they can, off of their friends. If it ain't raised after a year, you kill them. That's the general way. Only you don't kill the women. You keep them prisoner. They're always rich and beautiful. You take their watches and things, but you always take your hat off and talk polite. After the women have been with you awhile, they fall in love with you. That's the way it is in all the books."

"It sounds better 'n bein' a pirate."

"It's good, too, 'cause it's close to home and circuses and all that."

By this time everything was ready. The boys entered the hole, Tom in the lead. They worked their way to the tunnel's far end, tied their joined kite strings fast, and moved on. A few steps brought them to the spring. Tom shuddered. He showed Huck the fragment of candle wick perched on a lump of clay against the wall. He described how he and Becky had watched the flame struggle and go out.

Tom and Huck went down another corridor until they reached a steep clay hill about twenty feet high. Tom said, "Now I'll show you something, Huck." He held his candle up. "Look as far around the corner as you can. Do you see that—

there, on the big rock over yonder, done with candle smoke?"

"It's a cross!"

"'Under the cross,' Injun Joe said. Remember? Right yonder's where I saw Injun Joe raise his candle!"

Huck stared at the mystic sign, then said with a shaky voice, "Tom, let's git out of here."

"What? And leave the treasure?"

"Yes, leave it. Injun Joe's ghost must be nearby."

"No it ain't, Huck. It would ha'nt the place where he died, at the mouth of the cave, five mile from here."

"No, Tom. It would hang around the money."

Tom began to fear that Huck was right. Then he had an idea. "Look here, Huck, we're bein' fools. Injun Joe's ghost ain't gonna hang around where there's a cross."

"I didn't think of that," Huck said with relief. "Lucky for us that cross is there. Let's climb down there and hunt for the box."

Tom went first, leaving deep footprints in the clay hill as he descended. Huck followed. Four avenues opened out of the small cavern in which the great rock stood. The boys examined three of them with no result. Near the rock's base they found a small recess with spread blankets, an old suspender, some pork rind, and the well-gnawed bones of two or three chickens. But there was no box. They searched and searched, in vain.

"Injun Joe said '*under* the cross,'" Tom said. "Well, this comes nearest to being under the cross. It can't be under the rock itself because that sets solid on the ground." They searched everywhere again and sat down, discouraged. Tom pondered. "Looky here, Huck. There's footprints and some candle grease on the clay on one side of the rock but not the other. I bet you the money *is* under the rock. I'm going to dig in the clay."

"That ain't a bad notion, Tom," Huck said with enthusiasm.

Tom's knife was out at once. Tom hadn't dug four inches when he struck wood. "Huck, you hear that?"

Huck began to dig and scratch. The boys soon uncovered and removed some boards that had concealed a natural crevice leading under the rock. Tom entered the crevice and held his candle as far under the rock as he could. But he couldn't see to the crevice's end. He proposed to explore. He stooped and passed under the rock. The narrow way gradually descended. Tom and Huck followed its winding course. Tom turned a short curve and exclaimed, "Huck, looky here!"

It was the treasure box. It occupied a snug little cavern, along with an empty powder keg, a couple of guns, two pairs of old moccasins, and a leather belt.

Huck's hands plowed through the coins.

"We're rich, Tom!"

"I always reckoned we'd get it. Say, let's not fool around here. Let's get out. Lemme see if I can lift the box." It weighed about fifty pounds. Tom could lift it, awkwardly, but couldn't easily carry it. "I thought so," he said. "*They* carried it like it was heavy that day at the ha'nted house. I noticed that. I reckon I was right to fetch the sacks along." The money soon was in two sacks, and the boys brought it up out of the crevice.

"Let's fetch the guns and things," Huck said.

"No, let's leave them there. They'll be just the thing when we go robbing. Let's go, Huck. We've been in here a long time. It's getting late, I reckon. I'm hungry, too. We'll eat when we get to the skiff."

They emerged into the clump of bushes, looked around cautiously, found the coast clear, and soon were lunching on the skiff. As the sun dipped toward the horizon, they got underway. Tom skimmed up the shore through the long twilight, chatting cheerfully with Huck. They landed shortly after dark.

"We'll hide the money in the loft of the widow's woodshed," Tom said. "I'll come up in the morning, and we'll count and divide it. Then we'll hunt up a safe place for it in the woods. Lay quiet and watch the stuff 'til I run and fetch Ben Taylor's little wagon. I'll be right back." Tom disappeared and soon returned with the wagon. He put in the two sacks, threw some rags on top of them, and started off, hauling his cargo behind him.

When the boys reached the Jones house, they stopped to rest. Just as they were about to move on, Hugh Jones stepped out and said, "Who's that?"

"Huck and Tom Sawyer."

"Good! Come with me, boys. You're keeping everybody waiting. Trot ahead. I'll haul the wagon for you. Why, it's heavier than I would've thought. Got old metal in it?"

"Yes," Tom answered truthfully.

"The boys in this town will spend more time hunting up six cents' worth of old iron to sell to the foundry than doing regular work for twice the money. Hurry along now."

The boys wanted to know what the hurry was about.

"Never you mind. You'll see when we get to Widow Douglas's."

Afraid that he was in trouble, Huck said, "Mr. Jones, we haven't been doin' nothin'."

Jones laughed. "Well, I don't know about that, but you've got no cause to be afraid. Ain't you and the widow good friends?"

"Yes, she's been good to me."

"Alright, then."

Huck and Tom soon were pushed into Caroline Douglas's drawing room. Jones left the wagon near the door and followed. The place was grandly lit. Everyone of any consequence in the town was there. The Thatchers, Harpers, and Rogerses were there. So were Aunt Polly, Sid, Mary, Reverend Sprague, the editor of the town newspaper, and many more, all dressed in their best clothes. Caroline Douglas received the boys as gladly as anyone could receive two such filthy beings. Tom and Huck were covered with clay and candle grease. Aunt Polly blushed red with humiliation. She frowned and shook her head at Tom. However, no one suffered half as much as the two boys.

By way of apologizing for them, Hugh Jones said, "Tom wasn't home when I went to get him. I stumbled on him and Huck right at my door, so I just brought 'em here."

"You did just right," Caroline Douglas said. "Come with me, boys." She took Tom and Huck to a bedroom and said, "Wash and dress yourselves. Here are two new suits of clothes—shirts, socks, everything. They're Huck's. Mr. Jones bought one outfit, and I bought the other. But they'll fit both of you. Put them on. We'll wait. Come down when you're all slicked up." Then she left.

Huck said, "Tom, we can slip out if we can find a rope. The window ain't high above the ground."

"Shucks! What do you want to slip out for?"

"I ain't used to that kind of a crowd. I can't

stand it. I ain't goin' down there, Tom."

"Oh, bother! It ain't anything. I'll watch out for you."

Sid appeared. "Tom, Auntie has been waiting for you all afternoon. Mary got your Sunday clothes ready, and everybody's been fretting about you. Say, ain't this grease and clay on your clothes?"

"Mr. Siddy, you jus' mind your own business. Why's everybody here, anyway?"

"It's one of the widow's parties that she's always having. This time it's for Mr. Jones and his sons, on account of that scrape they helped her out of the other night. I can tell you something else if you want to know."

"Well, what?"

"I overheard Mr. Jones tell Auntie a secret."

"What's the secret?"

"That Huck tracked the robbers to the widow's. Mr. Jones is gonna try to surprise everybody here tonight, but his secret ain't much of a secret *now*." Sid chuckled in a self-satisfied way.

"You told, didn't you?"

"Never mind who told."

"There's only one person in this town mean enough to spoil a surprise like that, and it's you." Tom cuffed Sid on the ear and gave him several kicks that sent him out the door.

Some minutes later Caroline Douglas's guests were at the dinner table, and a dozen children were propped up at little side tables in the same room.

At the proper time, Hugh Jones made a little speech in which he thanked Caroline Douglas for the honor she was bestowing on him and his sons. "But," he said, "there's another person whose modesty . . ." And so on and so on. He sprung his secret about Huck's share in the adventure with as much high drama as he could. Everyone pretended to be surprised. Caroline Douglas did a pretty good job of looking astonished. She heaped praise and gratitude on Huck. This made him so uncomfortable that he almost forgot the discomfort of his new clothes.

Caroline Douglas said that she intended to give Huck a home under her roof and see that he got an education. When the time came, she said, she also would give Huck enough money for him to start a modest business.

"Huck don't need it," Tom said. "He's rich."

The gathering responded to this apparent joke with awkward silence.

"Huck's got money," Tom said. "You needn't smile as if you don't believe it. I can show you. Just wait a minute." Tom ran outside. People looked questioningly at Huck, who was tongue-tied. Tom returned, struggling with the weight of his sacks. He poured the mass of gold coins onto the table. "There! What did I tell you? Half of it's Huck's, and half of it's mine."

The spectacle took people's breath away. All gazed. No one spoke. Then there was a unanimous call for an explanation. Tom told the tale, and the audience remained taut with attention. When Tom finished, the money was counted. It amounted to more than $12,000—more than anyone present ever had seen at one time.

Chapter 17

Tom and Huck's windfall made a mighty stir in the little town of St. Petersburg. It was talked about, gloated over, and glorified until many citizens' reason tottered under the strain of the unhealthy excitement. Every "haunted" house in St. Petersburg and neighboring towns was ransacked for hidden treasure—taken apart, plank by plank, and its foundations dug up. The ransacking was done by men, not boys—some of them, ordinarily quite reasonable people (as people go).

Wherever Tom and Huck appeared, they were gawked at, courted, and admired. Everything they said was treasured and repeated; everything they did was regarded as remarkable. The town newspaper published short biographies of the boys.

Caroline Douglas helped Huck by investing his money for him, at six percent interest. At Aunt Polly's request, Judge Thatcher did the same with Tom's money. Each boy now had a prodigious income: about $5 a week. It was just what

Reverend Sprague got. (No, it was what he was *supposed to* get; generally he couldn't collect it.) In those days $1.25 a week would house, feed, clothe, wash, and school a boy.

Judge Thatcher now had a great opinion of Tom. No commonplace boy would have gotten his daughter out of the cave, he said. When Becky told her father how Tom had taken her whipping at school, the Judge was visibly moved and declared Tom a noble, generous boy. Judge Thatcher hoped that Tom would become a great lawyer or soldier some day; he said that he would help Tom get admitted to the national military academy and, afterward, to the country's best law school.

His wealth, and the fact that he now was under Caroline Douglas's protection, introduced Huck into society. Actually, dragged him into it. His sufferings were almost more than he could bear. Caroline Douglas's servants kept him clean and neat, combed and brushed. They bedded him nightly in sheets that had no stain or hole that might have put him at ease. Huck had to eat with a knife and fork and use a napkin, cup, and plate. He had to study, go to church, and speak so properly that he nearly lost the ability to speak at all. Civilization's chains now bound him hand and foot. For three weeks he bravely bore his miseries. Then he turned up missing.

For two days Caroline Douglas, greatly distressed, hunted for Huck. Deeply concerned, the town searched high and low. They even dragged the river for his body.

Early on the third morning, Tom Sawyer wisely searched the empty barrels behind the abandoned slaughterhouse. In one of them, he found the refugee. Huck had slept there. He had just breakfasted on some stolen food. Now he was smoking his pipe. He was dirty, uncombed, and dressed in the same old rags that he had worn in the days when he was free and happy.

Tom told Huck the trouble that he was causing and urged him to return to Caroline Douglas's house.

Huck's face turned melancholy. "Don't talk about it, Tom. I've tried it, and it don't work. It ain't for me. I ain't used to it. The widder's good to me and friendly, but I can't stand them civilized ways. She makes me get up the same time every morning, and she makes me wash. Her servants comb me all to thunder. She won't let me sleep in the woodshed. I got to wear clothes that smother me. They don't seem to let any air through, and they're so fancy that I can't set down, lay down, or roll around anywheres. I got to go to church, and I sweat and sweat. I hate them sermons! I can't chew tobacco in there. I got to wear shoes all Sunday. The widder eats by a bell, goes to bed by a bell, and gits up by a bell. Everything's so reg'lar, a body can't stand it."

"Well, everybody does it that way, Huck."

"Well, I ain't everybody. I can't stand it, Tom. It's awful to be so tied up. And food comes too easy. I don't take no interest in it when it comes that easy. I got to ask to go fishing. I got to ask to go swimming. I got to ask to do anything. I started talking so nice that my mouth felt all funny. I had to go up into the attic and cuss awhile to put the right taste back into my mouth. The widder doesn't let me smoke, yell, or gape. She doesn't let me stretch or scratch in front of people. And"— Huck squirmed with special distaste—"she prays all the time! I never seen such a woman. I had to leave, Tom. I just had to. Besides, school's gonna start soon, and I'd 've had to go. I couldn't stand that, Tom. Looky here, being rich ain't what it's cracked up to be. It's just worry, worry, sweat, sweat, and wish you was dead. *These* clothes suits me, and this barrel suits me. I wouldn't ever 've got into all this trouble if it hadn't been for that money. Please, take my share of it along with yours. Just gimme ten cents once in a while—not often, 'cause I don't give a darn for something 'less it's sort of hard to git. Please go and beg the widder to let me be."

"Huck, you know I can't do that. If you'll try this thing just a little longer, you'll come to like it."

"Like it! The way I'd like a hot stove if I was to set on it long enough! No, Tom. I won't be rich. I won't live in some cussed smothery house. I like the woods, and the river, and barrels, and I'll stick to them. Blame it all! Just when we'd got guns and a cave and were all set to go robbin', this dern foolishness had to come and spoil everythin'."

Tom saw his opportunity. "Look here, Huck. Bein' rich ain't gonna keep *me* from bein' a robber."

"You mean it, Tom?" Huck asked joyfully.

"Sure I do. But we can't let you into the gang if you ain't respectable."

Huck's joy vanished. "Can't let me in? You let me be a *pirate*."

"Yes, but that's different. A robber is more high-toned than a pirate. In most countries they're high up in the nobility—dukes and such."

Huck was silent, engaging in a mental struggle. Finally he said, "Well, I'll go back to the widder for a month, and see if I can come to stand it, if you'll let me be in the gang."

"That's a deal, Huck! Come on. Let's go. I'll ask the widow to let up on you a little."

"Will you, Tom? If she'll let up on some of the roughest things, I guess I can smoke and cuss in private and maybe pull through that way. When you gonna start the gang?"

"Right off. Maybe we'll get the boys together and have the initiation tonight."

"The what?"

"Initiation—the swearing in. You swear to stand by each other and never tell the gang's secrets, even if you're chopped to pieces. You swear to kill anybody that hurts one of the gang."

"That sounds mighty good."

"The swearing's got to be done at midnight, in the lonesomest, awfulest place you can find. A ha'nted house would be best, but they're all ripped up now. And you've got to swear on a coffin and sign it with blood."

"Now, that's somethin'! It sounds a million times better than pirating!"

This story ends here. If I went much further, this history of a boy would be in danger of becoming a history of a *man*. When you write a novel about grownups, you know exactly where to stop—with a marriage. But when you write about children, you just stop when you think you've gone on long enough.

Most of the characters in this book are still alive—prosperous and happy. Someday it might seem worthwhile for me to continue the story of the younger characters, so that you can see what sort of men and women they became. Therefore, I won't reveal any more for now.

Afterword

About the Author

In *The Adventures of Huckleberry Finn*, Huck says of *The Adventures of Tom Sawyer*, "That book was made by Mr. Mark Twain, and he told the truth, mainly." And Twain did tell the truth—mainly. In his preface to *Tom Sawyer*, he wrote, "Most of the adventures recorded in this book really occurred," adding that Huck and Tom were "drawn from life." To a large extent, *Tom Sawyer* is autobiography, with Tom being Twain's boyhood self.

Twain was born Samuel L. Clemens in 1835 in Florida, Missouri. Like Tom Sawyer, he spent his boyhood in a small Missouri town (Hannibal) on the Mississippi River.

Young Sam resembled Tom in many ways, large and small. He, too, plastered down his naturally curly hair. He, too, hated going to school and church, played hooky, and often was hit by his teacher. Like Tom, Sam loved to swim, play on an island in the Mississippi, and secretly "borrow" small boats for river outings. Sam led a group of boys in games that included playing pirates and digging for treasure. He and Tom Blankenship, the model for Huck, would exchange "meow" signals before setting out on night adventures. Fond of pranks, Sam once tricked a number of boys into whitewashing a fence for him, just as Tom Sawyer does. And, just as Tom delights in tormenting Sid, Sam delighted in tormenting *his* younger, well-behaved brother, Henry. Once, when Henry pointed out the color of the thread with which Sam's shirt was sewn—a sign that Sam disobediently had gone swimming—Sam (like Tom) got revenge by pelting the tattletale with dirt.

Also like Tom, young Sam knew horror and tragedy firsthand. Sam and a companion once were lost in the large cave near Hannibal; by the time a search party came to their rescue, their last candle had nearly burned out. As a boy, Sam saw a man threaten a widow outside her house at night; he came, one night, upon the corpse of a man who had been stabbed and carried to the Clemens house; and he witnessed the stabbing of another man. When Sam was twelve, his father died.

To help support his family, Sam became a printer's assistant. A few years later he worked as a printer and writer for his older brother, Orion, who had bought a local newspaper. But Sam remained Tom Sawyer, the restless adventurer.

Before he was eighteen, he left his home state. He worked as a printer in New York City; then Philadelphia; then Keokuk, Iowa; then Cincinnati. Next he moved to New Orleans and became a Mississippi River steamboat pilot. When the Civil War began, he became a cavalry officer in the Confederate army—but only for two weeks. After that, he resigned and went to Nevada with Orion. Still hoping to find buried treasure, he tried gold-mining in California. That didn't last long either. Sam returned to Nevada, where he wrote news stories and humorous pieces for a small newspaper. Next he went to San Francisco, where he wrote for another newspaper.

In 1865, a New York City paper published "The Celebrated Jumping Frog of Calaveras County," which bore Sam's recently adopted pen name: Mark Twain. The name recalled Sam's steamboating days, when crew members had called out "Mark Twain!" to announce a safe water-depth of two (twain) fathoms. The story—and the name Mark Twain—gained almost immediate fame. Published four years later, Twain's first book, *Innocents Abroad*, also was a hit. It remains the best-selling travel book of all time.

Although Twain married in 1870 and soon was a father, he didn't settle down. At various times, he lived in other countries, such as England and Austria, and gave humorous lectures in far-off lands such as India, South Africa, and New

Zealand. He wrote numerous essays, short stories, and novels that quickly became classics, including *The Adventures of Tom Sawyer* (1876), *The Prince and the Pauper* (1882), and *The Adventures of Huckleberry Finn* (1885), which many consider the greatest American novel.

Today Twain is regarded as one of literature's greatest humorists. But even during his lifetime, he was an internationally renowned writer and public speaker—a familiar cigar-smoking, bushy-haired figure in a white suit. Twain also was highly respected by literary critics, scholars, and other authors. Before he died in 1910, he received honorary doctorates from two of the world's foremost universities: Yale and Oxford. The boy from Hannibal, Missouri had come a long way.

About the Book

The Adventures of Tom Sawyer is an adventure, crime, and mystery novel, with a bit of romance. The story includes buried treasure, a house believed to be haunted, a grave robbing, a planned assault, and a murder. Two children become lost in a cave; someone else dies there. As if all of this weren't enough, the book is *funny*. While taking us into dark places, it provides plenty of laughter to light our way.

With humor, Twain shows human shallowness and fickleness. For months Tom has wooed Amy Lawrence, thinking himself in love. But at first sight of lovely Becky Thatcher, he forgets Amy. "Now he worshipped this new angel." Just as Tom attempts to impress Becky by showing off, the Sunday-school superintendent, librarian, teachers, and students try to impress her father, "the great Judge Thatcher," because of his high social status. When Huckleberry Finn is penniless and homeless, most of the townspeople scorn and shun him. When he suddenly has wealth and a home with respectable Caroline Douglas, his company is instantly desirable. The picture is similar, but darker, with regard to Muff Potter. Wrongly charged with murder, he is despised and vilified. When he is cleared of the charge, "the fickle world took Muff Potter to its bosom and fondled him as lavishly as it previously had abused him."

Twain also pokes fun at human superstition

and irrationality. Tom and Huck believe in ghosts, devils, witches, and spells. To cure warts, Tom tells Huck, "you've got to go, alone, into the woods, where there's a stump with rainwater. Right at midnight, you back up against the stump, jam your hand in, and say, 'Barley corn, barley corn, spells of all sorts. Stump water, stump water, swaller these warts,' and then walk away quick, eleven steps, with your eyes shut, and then turn around three times and walk home without speaking to anybody. If you speak, the charm's busted." Adults are scarcely more reasoning. Aunt Polly firmly believes in quack treatments. "She subscribed to all the 'health' magazines that offered worthless advice on how to breathe, what to eat and drink, how to get into bed, how to get out of bed, how to exercise, and how to think," Twain mocks. "She never noticed that the magazines of one month usually contradicted everything said in the magazines of the previous month." After the townspeople learn that Tom and Huck found treasure in a "haunted" house, "many citizens' reason tottered under the strain of the unhealthy excitement." Treasure-seeking men—not boys, Twain emphasizes—proceeded to ransack "every 'haunted' house in St. Petersburg and neighboring towns."

In addition to deceiving themselves, Twain's characters deceive others. Tom frequently lies to and fools Aunt Polly. Tom and Becky repeatedly feign indifference to each other. Tom tricks other boys into whitewashing a fence for him. He pretends to have earned a Bible prize, pretends to be sick (in an effort to avoid school), even pretends to be dead (so that he can, among other things, attend his own funeral). More sinisterly, "Injun" Joe avoids arrest by wearing a disguise. Before that, he bears potentially deadly false witness against Muff Potter.

Potter's wrongful imprisonment represents another aspect of human society that Twain satirizes: a tendency to confine and oppress others. Society forces Tom to go to school, which Twain half kiddingly calls "captivity." For Tom, attending church is a misery of forced silence and forced immobility. He finds his Sunday clothes uncomfortably restrictive: "There was a restraint about cleanliness and whole clothes that galled him." At one point, he protests that he always is "being forced to do things." Huck is even less able to bear society's constraints. Under Caroline Douglas's supervision, he must use a plate, a cup, a napkin, and utensils when eating. "I got to wear clothes that smother me," he complains. "They don't seem to let any air through, and they're so fancy that I can't set down, lay down, or roll around anywheres." Twain jokingly sympathizes, "He had to study, go to church, and speak so properly that he nearly lost the ability to speak at all. Civilization's chains now bound him hand and foot."

To escape civilization, Tom and Huck flee to natural surroundings. But nature, too, has a dark side. Teeming with life, the Mississippi River also is a place where people drown. Jackson's Island seems a near-paradise in good weather but becomes terrifying at the height of a storm. Tom and Becky become trapped in the literal darkness of McDougal's Cave. "The children fastened their eyes on their bit of candle and watched it melt slowly away. At last the half-inch wick stood alone. They saw the feeble flame rise and fall, climb the thin column of smoke, linger at its top a moment, and then... utter darkness." In this darkness "Injun" Joe dies, "his face close to the door's crack, as if his longing eyes had been fixed, to the last moment, on the light and cheer of the free world outside."

Tom Sawyer doesn't avoid the darkness of violence and death: Joe plans to disfigure a woman and fatally stabs a man. But the book supplies abundant "light and cheer" to see us through.